The Basket Case

Also Published in Large Print
from G. K. Hall by Ralph McInerny:

Getting a Way With Murder
Rest in Pieces
Abracadaver

The Basket Case

A Father Dowling Mystery

Ralph McInerny

G.K. HALL & CO.
Boston, Massachusetts
1992

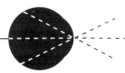

**This Large Print Book carries the
Seal of Approval of N.A.V.H.**

THE BASKET CASE. Copyright © 1987 by
Ralph McInerny.

Published in Large Print by arrangement with
St. Martin's Press.

G. K. Hall Large Print Book Series.

Printed on acid free paper in the United States of
America.

Set in 16 pt. Plantin.

Library of Congress Cataloging-in-Publication Data

McInerny, Ralph M.
    The basket case / Ralph McInerny.
      p.   cm. — (G.K. Hall large print book series)
  (Nightingale series)
    "A Father Dowling mystery."
    ISBN 0-8161-5569-0 (acid-free paper)
    1. Large type books.   I. Title.
  [PS3563. A31166.B3   1992]
  813'.54—dc20
                                    92-18387

To Mary and Pat Williams

One

The woman on the line spoke in a high nervous voice, and no wonder.

"Father, there's a baby in the church. In a back pew. Please take good care of him."

"A baby! Who is this?"

But the phone was dead. Father Dowling stared at the instrument a moment before returning it to its cradle. His impulse was to rush into the kitchen and tell Mrs. Murkin to go over to the church and see if there was indeed a baby in a back pew, but it was the housekeeper's imagined reaction that stopped him. He must proceed calmly. This meant getting up slowly, taking another puff or two on his pipe, and considering that the phone call was most likely a hoax. It would not be the first time someone had called a rectory to have a little fun with the priest. "How much are indulgences?" "What does an annulment cost if one isn't a Hollywood star?" Mrs. Murkin

1

would be shocked into angry huffing; Father Dowling found it more effective to ask how much the caller could afford.

But he did not think the woman who had just called was pulling a stunt. Her voice had been close to hysteria. He slipped out the front door of the rectory, paused to knock his pipe against the heel of his shoe, then walked to the church as swiftly as he could without actually running.

On this May afternoon, bright with sun, the air still fragrant with the smell of lilacs, the church itself seemed a springtime place. Sun streaming through the windows cast chips of color over the pews, creating a reasonable facsimile of flowers. As he hurried down the aisle, Father Dowling passed in and out of half a dozen such shafts of borrowed springtime. The basket was in the second-to-last pew on the Blessed Virgin's side, out of sunlight.

It might have been one of Marie Murkin's clothes baskets, placed sideways in the pew. His first impression was that it was filled with clothes. Baby clothes. But then he saw the puckered little face, a shock of coal-black hair, eyes seemingly squeezed shut against the world. This was without a doubt a baby. How old? Roger Dowling was no judge, but it looked to be the vintage of those he baptized, which would make it very young indeed. He pulled back the blue cover from the little face. How large his hand was in comparison. The chubby little chin told him nothing. It was when he was rearranging the blanket that he saw the envelope. Blue as the blanket.

He put the envelope into an inside jacket pocket, looking around to verify his first impression that the church was empty. Had an outside door just closed? Now that he had actually found the baby, he did not want to leave it to check the door. The fragility and vulnerability of this little creature were overwhelming. Father Dowling turned toward the front of the church and the tabernacle. His prayer was as unusual as the situation.

"I don't know where this baby came from but he's here and I'm stuck with him and I am going to need all the help you can give me." Thinking better of it, he knelt and prayed with more reverence though not with less urgency. Then he stood, grasped the basket at both ends and carried the baby back to the rectory.

"What on earth!" Mrs. Murkin cried when she opened the kitchen door after he pressed the bell with his elbow. "I thought you were in your study."

"I had to pick up a baby."

"What are you doing with that basket?"

It was the penalty for kidding her so much. She simply had not registered the mention of the baby.

"Is this your basket?"

He put it on the kitchen table. Marie approached it, squinting in appraisal, looked into it and let out a cry.

"It's a baby!"

"I know."

"Where did you get it?"

"Someone left it in church."

Marie, her mouth literally hanging open, looked at the basket, at Father Dowling, and back at the basket.

"The poor little thing."

She opened up the blanket, reached in and brought out the baby. Father Dowling had to force himself not to stop her from doing this. In the basket, wrapped in its blanket, the baby had some protection, but out in the open air, wrapped only in a thin white cloth, it was hardly an armful for Marie. "The poor little tyke," she said, in unaccustomed tones, authoritative tones, and began to rock her burden gently. She

4

cast a sharp eye at the priest. "Now, tell me where you got him."

"It is a foundling. I got a call saying the baby was there and I went over and that is what I found."

"Abandoned!"

"We can't keep it."

For a moment, he thought she was going to contest this. "Was it the mother who called?"

"It was a woman."

"Captain Keegan will know what we should do."

But Roger Dowling wanted to read whatever was in the thick envelope that had come with the baby before he did anything further.

"Can you take care of the baby for a few minutes?"

She just looked at him, as if to say, "Is the Pope Polish?" Of course she could look after the baby. She was a woman, was she not?

In the study, the priest refilled his pipe and put a match to it. This brought his arms together and he could feel the envelope nudging against him. Once he opened it, he would be committed. But what was the alternative? Turn the baby and the unopened envelope over to the police, or whomever Phil Keegan would tell them was the proper receiver of abandoned babies? Unthinkable. The letter was addressed to him, to a priest, and he could not disclaim responsibility. He remained standing while he slit open the envelope and took out what looked to be half a dozen folded sheets of the same blue as the envelope. He unfolded them and read the printed legend a the top of the page—CONSTANCE FARLEY RUSH. The priest lowered himself abruptly into his chair.

Dear Father Dowling:
    If you are reading this you have answered my cry for help and found my baby. Please tell no one what has happened. Above all, do not contact the police. Please. I am counting on you to take care of Timmy discreetly, I don't care what story you tell, only keep him safe and sound. And don't let anything I do or say in the next few days matter. You will know the real truth. Father, I can't thank you enough.

Would he have been able to make out the scrawled signature as Constance Farley

Rush if the name had not been printed at the top of the page? It was printed at the top of three blank sheets too. It seemed an odd waste of stationery.

His pipe, insufficiently drawn on in the surprise of the letter, had gone out. Roger Dowling relit it more carefully, still unsure what he would do.

Where the baby came from was no longer a mystery, and all he had to do was telephone Mrs. Rush and ask what was going on. He might not call the police, because she asked, but the letter said nothing about telephoning her. Nothing explicit. But if it wasn't implied, there was little reason for this indirect way of getting a baby into the hands of the pastor of St. Hilary's parish in Fox River, Illinois.

When he did pick up the phone, it was to call the former parish school, where Mrs. Hospers was in charge.

"Edna, how busy are you?"

"How busy is a one-armed man using dental floss?"

"You can't come over now?"

"It sounds like an emergency."

"Is an abandoned baby an emergency? Don't say anything if you're not alone."

"I'll be right over."

It was amazing how people could change their schedule when a baby was involved. Edna Hospers was the obvious solution for the baby. Had Mrs. Rush known that?

"A funny thing," Marie said in the doorway of the study. "I'd heard of them but I never saw them before."

"What?"

"Paper diapers."

"I will leave all that in your capable hands," Roger Dowling said hurriedly.

"It's a boy."

"Congratulations."

She closed one eye. "A less charitable person than I am would wonder. A baby being left for you, and all."

The priest only smiled. He was old enough to be the baby's grandfather, perhaps, but that is not an indictable offense, as Phil Keegan would put it.

"Mrs. Hospers is on her way over."

An expression of wounded jealousy came and went on Marie's face.

"I was going to suggest her. What shall we call him?"

"Moses. Is that basket yours?"

"No. It's brand new."

"So is the baby. Isn't he?"

"If he's a month old, I'd be surprised."

8

The front door burst open and Edna Hospers came running down the hall. She came to a stop next to Marie, breathing heavily. She looked excitedly at Roger Dowling.

"Where is he?"

"The nursery is in the kitchen."

——Two ——————

Mrs. Hospers, enthralled as she was with the baby, couldn't figure out what was really going on. Marie Murkin was either a whole lot dumber than past experience suggested, or she knew less than she pretended to.

"But where did he come from?" Edna held the baby close against her. What memories that brought back.

"Now, Edna, you know where babies come from."

"I do when I know the parents."

"Someone left that little fellow in the church," Marie said, shaking her head and reaching out to pat the baby's bottom. "Left him in that basket over there."

"And Father Dowling just happened to find him?"

9

"In a back pew, he said, just lying there, quiet as can be. Will you look after him, Edna?"

"You're giving him to me?"

"Father said he was sure you'd look after him until we learn more.

"Have you called the police?"

"Isn't that the thing to do?"

Why did she have the feeling that there was a lot more going on here than met the eye? Edna shook her head as if to clear it. Did she imagine Father Dowling was doing something wrong and wanted her to be an accomplice? That was as crazy as leaving a baby in the church.

"Someone telephoned and said the baby would be there," Father Dowling told her when he came into the kitchen. "A woman."

"It had to be the mother."

"Well, the mother had to be a woman."

"The poor thing. What would drive a woman to abandon her baby?" Edna shuddered at the thought. Once in Marshall Field's, little Eugene had gotten separated from her; it was during the Christmas rush, and an hour passed before she was reunited with him. His eyes were dry but very wide, as if he had just seen some side of the world he had not known existed. She had felt the same way. Is there an invisible umbilical cord that is never cut, linking mother and child forever? She did not find the thought at all repellent, although she looked forward to the time when her kids would be grown and embarked on their paths in life. That reunion with little Eugene was etched in her memory. The joy and relief, but the sense too of being somehow at fault. The security people had looked at her askance, as if they knew all about women who lose their kids while shopping.

"Jesus is found in the temple," Edna said.

Marie Murkin lurched and Father Dowling looked puzzled.

"That's my favorite joyful mystery. When Mary and Joseph find Jesus in the temple after missing him for days."

"Three days," Marie Murkin said, then glanced at Father Dowling to see if that was right.

"That is how she'll feel when she gets this little fellow back," Edna said.

"She didn't lose him," Marie said. "She left him."

"Even so." Edna turned to Father Dowling. "Did you call the police?"

"I didn't want to bother them with this yet."

"Bother them!"

"A bad choice of words. You're right." She loved his gentle voice and sharply etched profile. He reminded her of someone, she didn't know who. And how could she forget all that he had done for her and the kids? She would walk on hot coals for Father Dowling.

"I mean, it's their job."

"But not yet. I haven't told you everything. I can't yet. I'm asking a lot, I know. If you'd rather not look after him . . ."

"Do you know who he is?" Marie asked him.

"Moses?"

"Hmph. The mother. I'll bet you recognized her voice and you want to talk to her before the police do."

He would rather leave the police out of it altogether, Edna guessed. And she found herself agreeing.

"Whatever the reason, I would love to look after him. How long will it be?"

"I have no idea, Edna. But I can't imagine it will be for very long."

"It doesn't matter. Once I get him home I'll want to keep him."

"You can leave him with me during the day," Marie offered, but Father Dowling frowned.

"I'd rather you took the time off and kept him at home."

Edna did not like that. Next to her kids, her job at St. Hilary's was the most important thing in her life. She hated missing a day, and vacations were no treat for her. She took one for the sake of the kids; they had to go somewhere for a change, and just sending them to camp was not enough. It was a very difficult thing to have her husband and their father in prison. What was most worrisome was that they never seemed even to ask about him. She had broached the possibility of taking them to Joliet for a visit but Gene had vetoed that. Thank God. He could not hate the thought of his kids seeing him in there any more than she did.

Work made it possible for her to get through this. It was important that she not dwell on the fact that she was spending vital years of her life alone, without Gene. It was like being a widow, except that a widow can get interested in other men. Someone had suggested divorce to her, but that was out of the question. Annulment?

How could she kid herself that she and Gene were not really married? She had taken him for better or for worse. There had been a lot more worse, that was all.

If she did not balk at the prospect of staying at home, it was because this infant seemed such a godsend. Holding the warm little guy tight against her, she was willing to make sacrifices for him. Only it wouldn't be just a sacrifice. With him in her arms, she felt the thrill of fulfillment she had known the first time she held one of her own.

And so it was agreed.

"You can go home now, if you like."

The baby seat law couldn't apply to little Moses. Edna would just put the clothes basket in the back seat and he would be safe as . . .

"In church," Marie said drolly.

"I'd help you," Father Dowling said, but she stopped him.

"You can't wait to get him out of here, can you? Well, I suppose a baby in a rectory is a potential scandal."

"I don't think he has a vocation."

Marie said, "Moses without a vocation?"

"You just made up the name Moses, right?"

"It seemed to fit, Edna."

"I suppose he has to be called something."

"Don't you like Moses?"

"It makes him sound like a basketball player."

"Call him Aaron then."

"He played baseball," Marie said, and Edna got out of there. Both the pastor and the housekeeper seemed a little giddy with a baby in the house.

——Three ————————

Constance Farley Rush did not live in St. Hilary's parish—like most younger couples, she and her husband had moved to the suburbs—but both the Farleys and the Rushes had been longtime parishioners. The only Rush still alive was an octogenarian uncle of the baby's father, but Constance's mother and sister still lived in the house that had been the Farley family home for generations. The young Rushes, who were in their early thirties, lived in Barrington—in the town, not in one of those awful new developments. Constance had told him this in a waiting room at the hospital, during her convalescence from delivering her baby by cesarean section. Mrs. Farley, without actually asking him, had made it clear she thought a visit from Father Dowling would do her daughter a world of good. The golden-haired Connie, who was a chain-smoker, greeted him in her deep voice.

"It's better than drinking," she said, and his reaction made her add, "Oh, I don't mean me."

"I thought you meant me."

She thought it was a joke and there seemed no reason to correct her impression. He had gotten over his drinking, thank God, and then he had been assigned to St. Hilary's. Not so long ago, but now Father Dowling and St. Hilary's went together, according to the Cardinal, like Augustine and Hippo.

"We even have a potomus."

The Cardinal clearly would have preferred having the last MOT.

Connie said, "I meant my husband."

"Oh. I've never met him."

"That's one of the reasons."

"I might be of help to him."

"Who needs help?" she asked. Apparently she was mimicking Peter Rush.

It had been their only conversation, really, there in the visiting room, but hospitals bring forth confidences, and he felt he knew a good deal about her after spending thirty minutes and five cigarettes with her. Five of her cigarettes to his half pipeful. She really should cut down.

"I will when I'm pregnant again. I'm making up for the cigarettes I didn't have during these last months."

Mrs. Farley, Connie's mother, was not all that much older than Roger Dowling, but somehow he felt she belonged to an earlier generation. She was a handsome woman with what seemed a natural tan, thick hair the color of silver, cut fashionably short now. She was resigned to widowhood, a bit of a valetudinarian, as if surviving her husband were a kind of infidelity. She came to the noon Mass every day and on weekends brought along her unmarried daughter, Liz, who had silver hair like her mother's. Father Dowling's assumption that Liz was much older than Connie was quickly corrected.

"Liz could have married many times," Mrs. Farley assured him. "She should have married. She will deny it, but I am sure I am the reason she hasn't. She's given up everything to look after her aging mother." An idea the aging mother obviously did not find wholly distasteful.

The day little Timothy was left in a basket in the church, Father Dowling, having seen Edna Hospers off with the baby, decided to drop in on Mrs. Farley.

His excuse, if he could use it without sounding accusing, would be that she had not been to Mass that day. But it was Liz, not her mother, who answered the door.

"Is something wrong with your mother?"

Not the smoothest opening, but the mother's absence from Mass and now her daughter's presence at home on a weekday suggested something was amiss.

"So you've heard, Father?"

"As a matter of fact, I haven't. Is there anything I can do?"

"It's Connie who needs help, but of course she wouldn't take it from you."

He had gone ahead of her into the living room and turned, about to tell her to begin at the beginning, but she sensed his confusion.

"It's Connie's baby, Father. He's been kidnapped!"

"Good heavens. When did this happen?"

"Earlier today. But let Mother tell you.

18

It will do her good, just talking about it with you."

Mrs. Farley was at the back of the house, in a breezeway her husband had built between the house and the three-car garage. She had wanted a gazebo but settled for the breezeway. This little story was part of her standard repertoire. Roger Dowling had heard it at least three times before, but she told it with such grace he did not mind. She claimed to spend six months of the year sitting in the breezeway, reading, crocheting, watching television on a portable set that was never moved.

The television was not on today, nor was any book or needlework in evidence. Mrs. Farley sat forward in her chair, hands gripping its arms, staring straight ahead at some nameless horror. She was startled when Roger Dowling joined her, announced by Liz, who said she would leave them alone.

"You should go to the office," her mother said to her daughter, looking at Father Dowling for an ally. "Did Liz tell you about little Timothy?"

"She thought you would want to tell me."

"My grandson has been kidnapped."

"When did this happen?"

She looked at her watch. "It is nearly

19

four-thirty now. It happened three hours ago."

It had been more than three hours since Roger Dowling received the phone call. He had come from the church, had his lunch and gone to his study, where he lit his pipe in anticipation of an hour and a half with Dante.

"Tell me what happened."

It was a very detailed account, however brief. Mrs. Farley dwelt on the way Connie had left the baby in the car, rather than unbuckle the car seat and take Timothy out just to run in for some dry cleaning. Until a few months ago, the dry cleaner had had a drive-up window, but it had not proved the convenience it was meant to be.

"She wasn't away from the car three minutes, Father. But when she came back, the baby was gone."

She could not keep the tremolo from her voice, and Roger Dowling's heart went out to her. But he felt anger too, thinking of the basket left in the church and the infant now in the care of Edna Hospers. He wished he could tell Mrs. Farley her grandson was all right. What was Connie doing to her mother? In her note she had asked him not to wonder at what she might say about her missing baby. Obviously she had been referring to this fictitious kidnapping. She could not ask him to aid and abet such deception. He must see her at once.

"Where is Connie now?"

"She is upstairs in her room."

"Her room?"

A wintry smile. "I still think of the bedrooms as belonging to the children who used them. And I call my bedroom ours. They are habits I've never wanted to break."

"I understand. I'd like to see Connie."

Mrs. Farley frowned. "She isn't like Liz, you know. She doesn't practice her faith." Something occurred to her. "Thank God I nagged her until she had Timothy baptized. She would have left him a little pagan."

"I'd rather not go upstairs."

"Of course not. I'll have Liz get her. You can imagine how distraught Connie is."

"Yes."

As they waited, he wondered what Connie's reaction would be when she heard he was downstairs. In a minute Liz was back, a pleased if paled expression on her face.

21

"I was afraid she wouldn't want to see anyone, Father."

"Where can we talk?"

"Connie suggested the sewing room."

He followed her to a room between the kitchen and dining room, a converted pantry almost crowded with a sewing machine, a small desk, and a frilly stuffed chair.

Connie waited with one foot inside the door and one outside. She took his hand—her eyes studying him—and, when Liz left, she pulled him into the sewing room. As soon as she shut the door, she asked in a fierce whisper, "What did you say to Mother?"

"I was told a rather lurid tale."

"You didn't tell her the truth?"

"No."

"Why did you follow me here?"

He tucked in his chin. "I came to see your mother. I had no idea you would be here."

Connie's hair was cut in such a way that though she tossed her head frequently, it always reassumed the shape the cutting gave it.

"Why did you want to see Mother?"

"Connie, you are the one who has some explaining to do, not I."

"Not yet."

"Now. I will not collude with you. Can't you see what this is doing to your mother?"

"That's why I came here."

"When did you get here?"

"A few hours ago."

"Two-thirty?"

"Earlier. Is Timothy all right?"

Her maternal concern seemed belated. "Your baby is in good hands."

"Your housekeeper?"

"No. Mrs. Hospers."

"Who is she?"

"Connie, you entrusted your baby to me. I have taken care of him. Why did you tell your family he was kidnapped?"

"I also told the police."

Father Dowling was seated uncomfortably in a little chair with pale yellow covering. "You actually reported a kidnapping to the police?"

"Yes."

"It will be in the papers, Connie. On television."

"I hope so."

"Surely the police want to see you?"

"I told them I was going into hiding."

"Hiding?"

"All I need is two days."

"For what?"

She had put a hand on the wheel of the sewing machine and now moved it back and forth, causing the needle to drop, then rise again. "It's better you don't know."

"It is essential that I know."

She smiled. "It was your attitude toward the law that convinced me you were the one to trust. Don't let me down."

His attitude toward the law? What did she take him for? He was capable of paeans of praise for the law. He imagined Phil Keegan listening in and thinking, *Aha, at last. Roger Dowling reveals his true colors.* But more important than his attitude toward the law—it might have been Thomas More's—was the inadvisability of having a discussion with a woman about to lose control.

And that is how Constance Farley Rush struck him. No mystery there, certainly, not when you thought of what she had been up to since lunch. Dropping off her baby at church, telephoning the rectory, calling the police to report a kidnapping, and then coming here where she could not ignore the toll her story was taking on the baby's grandmother. Connie would have to be made of granite to get through all that unscathed. He quelled his annoyance and re- minded himself he was a priest.

"Trust me," she pleaded, tossing her hair.

"I have been doing that for some hours now. It was very unwise of you to tell the police your child was kidnapped. What do you suppose they will be thinking when they have to hunt for you?"

"I don't care for the police any more than they care for my baby."

"How many policemen do you know?"

"I suppose you know lots of them."

"Some of my best friends . . ."

She smiled. "Are kidnappers."

"Why kidnapping?"

"Because that is just what would have happened if I had not done what I did."

"Who would have kidnapped him?"

"His father. We are legally separated." A toss of her head. "Divorced, actually. I thought everyone knew." A little laugh. "I know that's crazy, but that is how my life has been lately. Since my father died." She paused and looked at him, as if about to revive memories of their talk in the hospital, but decided against it. "When your life be- comes a three-ring circus, you just assume everyone has a good seat. Thank God Daddy did not live to see this. It's bad enough putting Mother through it. But I guess Daddy saw it coming."

"Is this room too small to smoke a pipe in?"

"I'm so keyed up I forgot to smoke. Go ahead." She plunged a hand into her bag and brought out cigarettes. She got one lit in a practiced motion before Roger Dowling had begun to fill his pipe. He put it unlit in his mouth when Connie exhaled and the little room seemed suddenly full of smoke.

He said, "Before the police come, why don't you tell me all about it."

—— Four ——————————

Phil Keegan had liked the Fox River Police Department a lot better when he joined it than he did now, and the same went for its detective division, which he headed. Everything had become too damned big, with everybody knowing more and more about less and less. Police departments had to grow because of the rise in crime, that was the argument, and it sounded like a good example of a bad argument. Or so Roger Dowling had assured him over the cribbage board.

"It's like saying if welfare really did the job, the problem would be solved."

The priest smiled sweetly at the detective. As well he might. That was one of Phil's gripes.

Phil assured himself before the shaving mirror the following morning that it was a false parallel. He would tell Roger that. Better not. The pastor of St. Hilary's had an annoying way of getting the last word in such exchanges.

In the good old days the whole department would have pitched in when an alleged kidnapping hit them, but no more. Robertson actually asked who was in charge of kidnappings.

"Usually the kidnappers."

Robertson let it go. "Captain Keegan, a woman calling herself Constance Farley Rush phoned to say her baby had been kidnapped from a parked car."

"Connie Farley?"

"Do you know her?"

"I knew her father," Phil said. "My girls were friends of Connie's." Connie had stayed in Fox River, but both of Phil Keegan's daughters lived half a continent away. That fact, plus the death of his wife, made for a lonely existence. Father Dowling's assignment to St. Hilary's a few years back had been a lifesaver. He had known Roger even before he had met his wife.

"I want you to take charge, Captain Keegan." Robertson rearranged some papers on his desk. They seemed the same papers that had been there a week ago, and the week before that.

"Sure, I'll take it."

"You're in charge of kidnappings, aren't you?"

"Just so you meet my demands."

Robertson handed Phil a sheet of paper, and that sent Keegan downstairs to talk with the illiterate who had taken the message. It turned out to be a lovely redhead vaguely reminiscent of his eldest daughter.

"Sweetheart' send me up a transcript of this call, will you?"

"'Sweetheart, is not a rank in the police department," said a voice beside him.

He turned to face the mock feminist frown of Agnes Lamb, the newest member of his division.

"If it were, you know what Robertson's would be."

Agnes tried out several possibilities on the elevator going up, none of them lady-like. Keegan's enemies—and some of his friends—thought of the captain of detectives as a racist. There were days when that is how he thought of himself. But he knew that Agnes Lamb was the best thing to hit the Fox River Police Department in years, and she was undeniably black. She liked calling attention to that fact, but that was all right with Phil Keegan; he might have felt the same way in her shoes. When they worked together she was just a cop to him, and that was the highest praise he knew.

"We have a kidnapping."

"Alleged?" she asked prettily.

"What other kinds of crime do we deal with? This came in by phone. From the alleged mother of the alleged baby. I knew her father."

"The baby's?"

"Him too. But I meant the mother. I want you and Cy to check it out." Cy Horvath was a lot better than Agnes, but then he had been with the department longer, absorbing the wisdom of Phil Keegan.

"I thought you knew the lady."

"You'll like her."

Agnes read the garbled note the sweetheart downstairs had taken. "Rush? Are we maybe talking about the loving couple of the Rush divorce case?"

29

"The same. Their child."

"Maybe someone wanted to see if the kid is human or takes after its father."

Cy just nodded when told that he and Agnes were on it. Did it remind him of the Kornfeld case three years ago? That was the trouble with growing old, everything reminded you of something else. And everybody seemed to be the kid of someone you had known but was now dead. Why should Cy remember the Kornfeld case?

The transcript of the call made a little more sense than the redhead's note. Meanwhile, Agnes got on the phone to the Rush residence. No answer.

"It doesn't say where she was calling from."

"The dry cleaner's?"

Cy shrugged. The baby had been taken when she was in the dry cleaner's at Fenwick Mall. "Let's go see."

Cy was built like an NFL linebacker; Agnes was two-thirds his height and half his weight. Cy might have been running interference for a very small quarterback when they left the office.

Keegan lit a cigar, picked up his phone but did not punch a button. He was remembering Harold Farley.

The Farley house was just two blocks over from the one in which Phil had raised his own family, the house he had sold when it became too much trouble, but mainly because of the memories it evoked. Harold Farley had lived out his life in the house where he brought up his kids. His widow was still there; and the daughter who hadn't married lived with her mother.

Keegan liked that, a daughter putting her mother first, except that it sounded like criticism of his own daughters, so he pushed the thought away. People should lead their own lives. Now he seemed to be criticizing the Farleys for thwarting their older daughter's life. What was her name anyhow? He would think of it. The other girl had married and her husband led her a helluva life, and now this, her baby kidnapped. There was the very messy divorce that had been contested unsuccessfully by Connie. Maybe Mrs. Farley would have both her daughters back now, and her grandchild too, before it was all over. The St. Hilary connection made the whole thing kind of cozy. So what if he had the added satisfaction of providing police services to people he had known all his life? He was already looking forward to telling Roger Dowling about this.

But back to Harold Farley. He had stayed in the family house, although with the money he made he could have lived any-where, as in the story of the four-hundred-pound gorilla. Harold had been a dapper little man, camel-hair coat, a homburg. Silk scarf, too, in winter, and in summer wing-tipped shoes, maybe a glen-plaid suit, solid tie. His mustache was full, his hair silver. He and his wife might have been twins as they grew old together. Wasn't that the the-ory, a man and his wife come to look more and more alike? Or was it a man and his dog? Harold Farley had had a basset hound, a series of them, getting a puppy when their dog grew old, starting over again. The way some men do with wives. But Harold Farley had been a devoted husband.

They had always been a sight, the Farleys, coming to the ten o'clock Mass at St. Hilary's every Sunday, he escorting his family down the aisle before assuming his usher duties, slow, very dignified, the two lovely girls following. Good Catholic, Har-old Farley. A Knight of Columbus, of course, but he was also a Knight of St. Gregory, a special honor from the Pope himself. Did Father Dowling know there had been a Knight of St. Gregory in the parish? Think of that. They had actually known about St. Hilary's parish in Rome. But it was the obscurity of the parish Roger liked and Phil was all for that. He didn't want the Cardinal wondering why he was wasting a priest like Roger Dowling in Fox River. Maybe he and Roger would buy a condominium in Florida for their old age. If they had one. Harold Farley had died with his boots on, and that was the best way if you could manage it.

The story was that Farley had made his money in the stock market. That made sense. Harold came to his pharmacy every day and went to the office in back but he never appeared behind the prescription counter. Wore a suit all day, had several telephones. Nowadays he would have had a computer, Phil supposed, not that he himself knew anything about the market. He was as likely to buy hog futures or a ticket in the daily double at Arlington as he was to buy stock.

Success had taken Harold Farley from the back of the drugstore downtown to Farley Enterprises. All that money would have left the kids well off, Keegan supposed. But where there is money, there is trouble. Trouble like kidnapping, for example.

Constance Farley Rush was nowhere to be found. Cy Horvath and Agnes Lamb checked out the dry cleaner's and then went to the Rush residence in Barrington, drawing a blank at both places. Oh, they remembered the woman at the dry cleaner's. Came in on the run, picked up her things, left and was back like a shot. "My baby's gone! Someone took my baby from the car!" She called the police and then took off like a bat out of hell.

"I haven't heard that expression in years," Keegan said.

"I'm quoting the lady behind the counter."

Cy's voice, like Cy's face, told you nothing he didn't want you to know, and Keegan was left as always to wonder whether Cy was dumb or smart. The verdict was smart, based on a truly impressive record over the years. Did he know Cy any better now than at the beginning? Not really.

"I thought we'd check on the father."

"They've broken up."

"I know."

"Keep in touch, Cy."

"Agnes wants to talk to you."

"Put her on."

"Captain, I just want to ask when you're

putting me up for promotion to sweetheart."

"It just came back negative. Sorry,
Agnes."

Agnes said a nasty word and hung up.
Keegan got the dial tone and rang the number of the St. Hilary rectory.

"Marie, is Father Dowling there?"

"He would have answered the phone
himself if he was."

"Where is he?"

"Is this an official inquiry?"

"No, I'm just being nosy."

"Then I'll tell you. I don't know. He was
going to call on some parishioners, that's
all he said."

"And you'll find out who when he gets
back?"

"Now you *are* being nosy."

"Tell him I called. I might drop by later."

"Are you coming to dinner?"

"Is that an invitation?"

"I'm only the housekeeper. I can't give
invitations."

"Thanks. I'll be there."

Meanwhile he would go across the street
and have a boilermaker. He had quit drinking during lent and was still making up
for it.

—— Five ——

It was not often that Roger Dowling found a visit from Phil Keegan unwelcome, but on this occasion he did. Marie told him as soon as he returned from Mrs. Farley's and naturally expected him to be pleased.

"For dinner?"

"That's okay, isn't it?"

Of course it was. It was just that he did not relish the prospect of an evening of dissembling. He had no doubt the reported kidnapping would come up, and he would have to keep quiet about what he knew, even though they were things Phil had a right to know. Constance Farley Rush was using him and he did not like it, but for the moment at least he would go along with it. He only wished she were easier to believe. He had the feeling that if he could have a long unmonitored conversation with her sister Liz he would get a better idea of what was going on. Meanwhile, he had time before Phil's arrival to say some office and then review the events of the past several hours.

He still said his breviary in Latin, seeing

no reason to switch to English. Latin had been a favorite subject since he was thirteen years old. He would not go so far as to say that Latin was spoken in heaven, but it had been, and still was, the language of the Church. Not that he had anything against the liturgy in English. Far from it. He provided one Latin Mass a week for his parishioners, the new rite in Latin. It was simply too much of a hassle to get permission to say the Tridentine Mass.

Having said Vespers and Compline, he put aside the leatherbound volume, lit a pipe and had some long, long thoughts about Constance Farley Rush.

Her story was that she was preventing the kidnapping of her son by its father by reporting a fake kidnapping and hiding the baby.

"Do you expect your husband to be arrested?" he had asked.

"I just want to put the fear of God into him."

"This seems a complicated way to do that."

"Oh, you don't know him.

"But what will you have accomplished? How will you retrieve your baby?"

"Someone can leave him in a blanket

in your church and call you to say he's there."

He had to admire her nerve. She studied him through a cloud of exhaled smoke while she said it. Had she rehearsed this conversation as well? Maybe she had not thought to see him so soon, and at her mother's house, but he was sure some contact beyond the letter would have been made, and soon. So she would have planned a confrontation and here they were in the sewing room having it. He didn't like it.

"And when will I find the baby?"

"Tomorrow."

"You expect to avoid the police until the baby is found?"

"Yes."

"Will you tell them you were here?"

"I wouldn't lie about it." She said it with a straight face. "Anyway, no one will care then that they couldn't find me."

"They might think you've been kidnapped too."

Her eyes sparkled at the suggestion. That was one thing at least that had not occurred to her.

Phil was in a jovial mood when he arrived.

But then he had been in a good mood ever since the Bears won the Super Bowl. Roger Dowling almost regretted the triumph, wondering if he could ever feel the same about the Bears again. Chicago sports fans had been given abundant reminders of the unreliability of the things of this world. Who could put his trust in the temporal order when it was regularly betrayed by baseball, basketball, and football teams, wresting defeat from victory? It had been a spiritually salutary experience to be a fan in Chicago. Now, in the modest parlance of the NFL, the Bears were world champions. Somehow it did not seem right.

The one thing that could be said in its favor was that it had mellowed Phil Keegan.

"You know old Mrs. Farley?" Phil asked when Marie had brought him a beer and they were settled in the study.

"I had a visit with her this afternoon."

"What time?"

"Why do you ask?"

Phil thought a moment. "If you have to ask she didn't tell you, which means she didn't know."

A few puffs on the priest's pipe got them past that. As he spoke, Phil had turned the remark into a half question, as if second-guessing his assumption. Thank God he hadn't put it as a direct question. There are many ways of not answering a direct question, but Roger Dowling did not like using them on his old friend.

"Her grandson has been kidnapped."

"Good heavens."

"Hardly more than an infant."

"Tell me all about it."

"No, wait," Marie pleaded. "I want to hear too. Tell it at table."

They adjourned to the dining room, where Roger Dowling frowned at Marie. It was one thing not to tell Phil Keegan what they knew, to openly feign ignorance was something else. But the distinction would have been lost on Marie. Father Dowling had often thought his housekeeper would make a good canon lawyer. She had a knack for finding excuses for anything she really wanted to do.

"Well," Phil began, obviously pleased to have brought them such a story. "Let me start at the beginning."

It was interesting to see things from the police perspective, partial as that viewpoint necessarily was. Of course he had the unfair advantage of knowing things Phil did not.

"Has she received a ransom demand?"

"She hadn't when she reported it."

"And since?"

Phil's brow clouded. "The fact is we can't find Connie."

"Can't find her!" Marie cried, and this surprise at least was genuine.

"She's disappeared."

Marie stopped ladling soup. "Maybe she was kidnapped too!"

"Not very likely," Phil said.

"But where would she be?"

"She'll show up."

"I'll bet she's at her mother's," Marie cried.

Phil shook his head.

"Why not, Phil Keegan? Did you check?"

"I don't have to. Father Dowling paid her a visit today." He turned to Roger. "Was she there, Roger?"

"Mrs. Farley? Yes, we had a long talk. Don't ask me what about. In fact, let's just draw a veil over my visit to Mrs. Farley."

"But had she heard?" Marie asked.

"Marie," he said in a warning tone.

"Oh, for Pete's sake."

"Did you find the father, Phil?"

"Cy talked with him. Nothing. He hadn't heard from his wife. He guessed she had taken the baby to their cottage in Wisconsin."

"He thinks the kidnapping is fake?"

Keegan looked him in the eye. "So do I."

—— Six ——————————

Old Tom had a chiseled profile, a perpetual frown, and a mouth that was always half an inch open: the expression of a man who had been missing the point of jokes for three score and ten. Sometimes he thought there was a general conspiracy against Old Tom, but so far as he could tell they never got together to plan it, it just turned out that way. So it had been for the thirty years he put in on the railroad and, pensioned but still young, for the fifteen years he put in doing donkey work for judges at City Hall. The joke was always on him.

Until he began to spend his days at St. Hilary's, where the school had been converted into a haven for the retired. The new conspiracy was to treat Old Tom like everyone else, and he found *that* so confusing he became a kind of roving recluse.

He went to St. Hilary's every day, not really a part of it all, spending most of the time on his feet, avoiding potentially entangling involvements—some of those old dolls had ideas or he was crazier than he thought—and walking around. He liked to circle the block and come back to the school along the walk that ran between the church and rectory. That was how he happened to see the woman leave the basket in the back pew of the church.

He had come up the street and then slipped into the church, walking up and down the main aisle (not kneeling down, but he figured God knows a good intention). Then, hearing someone in the vestibule, Tom headed for the circular stairway that led to the choir, just to be out of the way.

Out of sight, he stopped. The woman was so close he heard her intake of breath when she got inside. The door closed, making a jerky squeaking sound as it did. It was another sound that made him peek. A baby? It was in the basket the woman carried, and from his angle he could see the infant.

That didn't surprise him, not at first; maybe he thought she was bringing it to be baptized, but when she hurried to a pew and then swiftly made for the door again, without the basket, Tom came scampering out of hiding. He didn't know what the hell was going on, but he didn't plan to be around when explanations were demanded.

He was outside, down the steps and moving up the sidewalk almost as quickly as the woman. That had been a mistake. She stepped into the street, opened the door of her car and turned. Their eyes met and there was no way in the world he could conceal the fact that he knew what she had just done, dumped a baby in the church.

But she was the one getting caught, not him. Her eyes rounded and for what seemed the longest time they stared at one another. Then apparently deciding he was no threat, she ducked into the car, slammed the door shut and pulled away. The motor had been running. However long or short a time they stared at one another, it had been enough. Old Tom knew he had seen that woman before.

Once she was gone, the question became what to do. He wanted to go back inside the church and make sure the baby was still there, but what if it was? He didn't know anything about babies. What he did was sort of hang around, protecting the kid, you might say, Old Tom on guard duty.

When Father Dowling came out of the rectory and headed for the church, Tom ducked behind a tree. The priest wasn't running but he was on the move, no doubt about that. What were the chances of his checking out the pews and finding the basket? Tom didn't like it. The only way was for the kid to start crying while the priest was in the church, but there hadn't been a peep out of it when . . . when Mrs. Rush wrestled the basket through two sets of doors.

He might have enjoyed realizing he had placed the woman if the priest hadn't come out of the church just then. And he had the basket with him! There was luck for you. And bad luck for the priest. What was he going to do with a baby in the rectory? And how would he know it was Mrs. Rush who left the baby?

Somehow it had just clicked, her face and the courthouse, and the way they had all kidded about the Rush divorce. First there had been the legal separation, with the divorce to follow on it automatically. Old Tom remembered it because she had put up a fight. She did not want a divorce. Which had made people at the courthouse wonder if she knew what a sonofabitch her husband was. Tom knew about unhappy marriages from personal experience.

Mildred was little more than a bad dream now, but it had gone on for twenty-two years and at the funeral everyone remarked how well he was taking it. He wished Mildred well in the next world, he had Masses said for her soul and all that, but he did not miss her one bit. She had spoiled the only kid they had, taught him to look down on his father. Tom hadn't seen Wilbert for five years, maybe more. That's how much it mattered. Maybe he should have married Rosemary Young. Life would have been different. But by the time he buried Mildred, Rosemary was long since happily married in Superior, Wisconsin. She sent a card, which was nice. He didn't think Rosemary thought her husband was a sonofabitch. If all the stories about Peter Rush were true, his wife would have had to be a saint or retarded to overlook it. And she wanted to hang on to him at all costs.

Wandering back to the school after Father Dowling had disappeared into the rectory with the basket, Tom put his mind to what he remembered of the Rush divorce. Everyone said she was the one with money, which took away one explanation of her reluctance, unless she feared *he* would ask for alimony. And damned if he didn't. Imagine that, a man asking a judge to force his divorced wife to support him. That alone was grounds for divorce, but he was the one asking for it, not her. Had she felt about the alimony request the same way the Sages of the Courthouse had? (Another equivocal memory. Tom had never been a recognized member of the Sages of the Courthouse. Perkins had said that, being so bowlegged, Tom ought to be a Rider of the Purple Sage instead. Laughter. What the hell did that mean?) In the end, Judge Molly Jones granted the sanofabitch alimony. Jones was a feminist, who pretended there was no difference between the sexes, but she had fined a drunk for stumbling into a women's restroom to take a pee. It figured. She had accepted Mrs. Rush's complaints about her husband spending more money than he earned, but considered depriving him of the opportunity to keep it up cruel and unusual punishment.

Now the injured party in the Rush divorce had left a baby in a basket in St. Hilary's church. Tom was thinking about that so hard he didn't have time to dart away and avoid a confrontation with Mrs. Hospers. But she just gave him a preoccupied smile and whizzed on past him on her way to the rectory.

Inside the school, on a hunch, Tom went up to the second floor and stood at the end of the corridor, looking out the window. There was octagonal mesh embedded in the glass because that had once been a playground down there, but he could see all right. His hunch paid off.

He had to press the side of his head against the window but he had a good view of Mrs. Hospers emerging from the rectory with a basket, which she put in her car and drove away.

What in Sam Hill was going on?

——— Seven ————————

That Mrs. Rush was not to be found at the dry cleaning store in the Fenwick Mall was no surprise, but Cy was disappointed that she had not headed home, a disappointment Agnes Lamb gave expression to.

"Damn. Well, where does her old man work?"

Cy checked downtown and got the word that Peter Rush kept an office in the Fenwick Mall. Convenient, but their being divorced made it unlikely she would have gone to him.

"Tell them tragedy unites," Agnes said. They heard her downtown, indistinctly, and asked Cy to copy again.

"Any ransom demand yet?" he asked.

"Negative."

"Let's try the Fenwick Mall," Agnes said.

"Again," Cy said.

"Yeah."

Just an observation. Mrs. Rush left her dry cleaning at the Fenwick Mall because it was close to the house in Barrington. No doubt that was why her husband's office was in the mall, too, rented before the big breakup.

The second floor of the central part of the mall contained offices, and there was a table of contents at the foot of the stairs. Peter Rush was in 2024.

"What is a financial consultant?" Agnes asked.

"A man who tells you how to get rich."

"And that's how he gets rich? No thanks."

They went up the stairs and along a low corridor to 2024. The plate on the door looked bronze but Agnes decided it was plastic. PETER RUSH. FINANCIAL CONSULTANT. The door was locked.

There was a dentist across the hall, a foot doctor on one side and an insurance agent on the other. The insurance agent's door was locked, too.

"Which do you want?" Cy asked.

"Dr. Peddy. Maybe I'll make an appointment."

The dentist's name was Dunn and he was in the reception room hovering over his receptionist when Cy came in. The dentist straightened and two perfect smiles were turned on Cy.

"Police," Cy said, watching the smiles fade. "We're trying to contact Mr. Rush across the hall."

"Now it's the police? Maybe I should try that."

"What do you mean?"

"To collect," Dunn said. "I put two thousand dollars' worth of bridgework into his mouth, so far for nothing."

"Have you seen him today?"

"I haven't seen him in weeks. But then he's avoiding me. June?"

June was bursting out all over in a starchy sort of way. "No, Doctor."

"Have you seen Mrs. Rush?"

"Mrs. Rush! They're divorced." Having said which, June looked significantly at the dentist, who ignored her.

"Something wrong, Officer?"

"How do you mean?"

"This is a bit odd, isn't it? Asking about a fellow tenant, then his wife. Are they missing?"

"What made you think that?"

"I didn't think it. I just asked a question. Pardon me all to hell." He turned to the receptionist. "When is my next appointment?"

She scanned what seemed to be an uncrowded page. "You have time to work on those castings, Doctor."

He pushed through a louvered door that swung twice and then subsided. June had her smile back on, but it conveyed no warmth.

Cy said, "Thanks for your help."

"Wait." She was whispering. Cy waited. She made a gesture, indicating they should go into the hall. Cy went out and she joined him.

51

"She was here, Officer. This morning. She was going out when I came in."

"When was that?"

"After ten. This is a slow day." She said it in such a way that Cy suspected it was a day like most others. How do dentists attract a clientele anyway? Dunn was young and probably thought this mall location was perfect. Maybe he would be proved right eventually. Meanwhile, idleness, and June, might get him into trouble.

"I wonder who locked the door?"

June took hold of the handle of Rush's door and pushed, hard. She had a businesslike air about her. Cy would not have been surprised if it had opened under the pressure.

She gave up. "It would lock automatically, more likely than not. We leave ours open all day. Of course we want to be noticed." She looked up and down the hallway with an ironic smile. "Winners Row."

"Isn't Rush doing well?"

"It all came out at the trial."

"How about Peddy?"

"How many people do you know with bad feet?"

"Plenty."

She laughed. "All cops I'll bet."

52

He had known the woman five minutes, and already there was a lack of barriers that verged on intimacy. Cy had the notion June could move in on a man, married or single, before he knew what was going on. Did she have designs on Dunn even though his offices were on Winners Row?

"Mrs. Rush say anything when you saw her?"

June didn't move but he had the feeling the distance between them had decreased. "She was walking pretty fast."

"You mean she didn't see you?"

"Let's just say I avoided her. I mean, all their troubles had become public. I didn't want to embarrass her." She was back again, apparently taken by this image of herself as a considerate human being.

"Hello, hello," Agnes said, swinging down the hall toward them. "Any news?"

"My partner," Cy explained. June was back to being a receptionist. In a moment she was back in the office behind her desk.

"Did I say something wrong?" Agnes asked.

"I'll tell you on the way to the building manager's."

"You found out something from Betty Boop back there?"

"How were things in feet?"

"Toe to toe."

The directory downstairs told them that inquiries about office rentals should be made to the mall manager, Henry "Hank" Guardino. They checked the map of the mall to locate him, at the end of one of the ganglia in a narrow corridor past the restrooms.

"Not a very nice neighborhood," Agnes said.

"Maybe he has bad kidneys."

There was enough of Henry "Hank" Guardino to contain dozens of ailments. He looked to be about 250 pounds to Cy, which on a frame of five and a half feet gave the impression of a grounded balloon. The name had sounded vaguely familiar to Cy and now he saw why. So this is where second-string professional football players ended up, managing malls. The fact that they were police did not bother Hank, not after Cy had complimented Guardino for playing on the best Bears team before television changed the game.

"Changed is right. When I hear what those guys are paid." Hank scrunched his eyes closed and shook his head slowly.

"You've got a tenant named Peter Rush."

"Maybe I do and maybe I don't."

"What's that mean?"

"That the sonofabitch owes me three months' rent. Sorry," he said to Agnes. "I'm supposed to throw him out on the street or what? I didn't count on any sonofabitches renting offices here. Sorry."

"When did you last see him?"

"I saw his ass end, sorry, about a week ago, heading across the lot to I suppose his car. He heard me. I know he heard me. My voice carries. But he just kept running. Sonofabitch."

"Sorry," Agnes said.

"You got a key to his office? We want to take a look."

"You got a warrant?"

"Just say we're acting for his creditors."

"Let's go."

Hank moved through the people in the mall as if he were heading for a goal line, his footwork still nimble despite the superstructure. Cy and Agnes let him run interference for them, impressed that Hank never touched anyone, let alone bowled them over.

He was twirling his key chain as he advanced down the hall to Rush's door. He swung it like a yo-yo when he reached the door, caught the keys and jammed one into the lock. Neat.

Hank stepped aside and Cy went in. Into the dark. He was fumbling for the switch when Hank reached in and turned on the light.

"Sorry."

"What did you say?" Agnes asked. Hank just looked at her. As Cy waited for them to come in, he wished Hank would leave them to it, but the old pro did not look that accommodating. He stood in the hallway, puffing, sweating, arms akimbo, as if waiting for something.

What must have been the receptionist's desk in the outer office was piled high with paper and boxes and folders. There was no typewriter. How long since someone had sat there?

The venetian blinds in the inner office were pulled and it was when he went to open them that Cy discovered the body.

By tripping over it. He put out his hand and made a great clatter with the blades of the blind. The light went on. Hank had flicked another switch. Agnes looked down at the mortal remains of Peter Rush lying on his side, the chair he had been sitting in toppled over. The blood that had run from his temple down his cheek had caked and dried.

"He's dead," Agnes said, as if warning herself never to take death too calmly.

Hank came all the way into the inner office and looked down at the body of his tenant.

"The poor sonofabitch," he said.

He did not sound sorry.

—— Eight ———————————

The body was discovered at 6:05 P.M. The call came to the rectory when they were still at table, where Phil was hearing everything Cy and Agnes had learned about the goings-on at the Fenwick Mall.

"A heart attack?" Roger Dowling asked hopefully when Phil put down the kitchen phone.

"Not until someone gave him a good hit on the head." Phil gave a quick account of the message.

"Oh, this is terrible," Marie cried. "First the baby, now this."

Father Dowling looked at her without particular expression. If she should blurt it out now, he would not be reluctant to

57

tell Phil about the baby in the basket. But Marie said nothing more. Not that it would have mattered, perhaps. Phil Keegan did not have time now to pursue a fake kidnapping.

"Come with me, Roger."

"I'd just be in the way."

Phil turned, his face wearing a lopsided grin. "Of course you'll be in the way. That never stopped you before."

"I don't want to wear out my welcome."

Phil's smile dimmed. Good Lord, had he taken it as a reference to his own frequent visits to the rectory? Roger got up and accompanied his old friend to the door. "Come back later, if you can, Phil. I'd like to hear the details."

Phil loped out to the car and, watching him go, the priest wondered if people appreciated what the police do in the line of duty. Phil Keegan was exceptionally devoted, of course, and recognized no firm distinction between being on duty and off. It could be argued that his life was so lonely that he needed police work to fill in the barren stretches of time when he would otherwise be alone. He did not, after all, spend all his time at St. Hilary's. In any case, the phone call put an end to

Marie's wondering what came first with Phil.

"Well, what do you make of that?" she asked, standing in the kitchen doorway, hands on her hips.

"Don't take it as a negative estimate of your cooking, Marie."

"What?"

"Duty called him. I thought he enjoyed the little he managed to eat before he had to go."

Marie looked as if she were going to stamp her foot. "You know what I mean. That poor little baby's father has been murdered. Someone seems bent on wiping out the entire family."

"I suppose the mother's next," Father Dowling said, tapping on his chin with the stem of his pipe.

"You don't really think so."

"Then the grandmother. Then anyone who had anything to do with the kidnapped baby."

"You're impossible! A person tries to have a simple conversation and you turn it into I don't know what."

It was a fault of which he often accused himself when he confessed, teasing Marie. It was a silly thing to do, sometimes almost mean. He reminded himself of his Aunt Ruth, who had been a merciless teaser, once convincing him that he had green hair that glowed in the dark and other nonsense. The only time he had seriously thought of running away from home was when his Aunt Ruth came for a visit. And here he was carrying on in her ignoble tradition. Why is it that the faults we abhor tempt us most?

He would make it up to Marie. But he knew her well enough to realize that an apology now would be taken as a continuation of his teasing. His mind turned to other things and he wondered if he should call the Farley house first or just drop by. He got his pipe going while he thought about it.

The day had been a strange one thus far and it was not yet over. The telephone call, the baby in the basket, pressing Edna into service, the visit to the Farleys.

Constance Farley Rush's ruse to preempt her husband's plan to kidnap their child had lost its point before she put it into play. Phil's information was that Rush had been dead for hours when he was found. How could one not wonder if that murdered husband did not explain what Connie had done with the baby?

The priest thought of the woman with whom he had talked that afternoon. Had she known at the time her husband was dead? Known because she was responsible for it?

A blow on the head to a seated man. The manner of Rush's murder posed no insuperable problem for a woman assassin. Father Dowling had lived long enough to know that anyone is capable of anything. Not out of the blue, perhaps, but the erosion that precedes the major moral lapse is seldom publicly visible. Characters dissolve much as they are built up, by a slow accumulation of seemingly unimportant deeds.

In the case of the Rushes, their troubles had become public, sign enough that much had intervened to alter whatever they had felt for one another when they pledged fidelity. It would not have been a blushing bride who struck her husband a fatal blow—if that was what had happened. And people do go on after committing such deeds. It was not at all impossible he had chatted in the sewing room with a woman whose husband's blood was fresh on her hands.

The doorbell rang before he had made

up his mind what to do. He let Marie answer. It was like making up to her. In a moment she came to the door of the study, her eyes surrounded by white.

"Elizabeth Farley, Father Dowling. She wonders if you would have a moment to speak with her."

She came in with her light blue raincoat billowing dramatically and did not wait for Marie to go before announcing, "My brother-in-law Peter Rush has been found dead."

The little yelp from Marie was genuine enough. Perhaps hearing the news from this prematurely gray, patrician young woman gave it more solidity than a police report.

"How did you find out?"

If his intention had been to answer surprise with surprise, he could not have done better. She sank into a chair and looked at Roger Dowling as if she had never really seen him before. "Is that your first reaction, how did I learn Peter is dead?"

"We just heard ourselves," Marie said, as if eager to save the pastor from shame. "Captain Keegan was here when he got the call."

"So you already knew."

"You haven't answered my question."

"Is it important?"

"Yes."

"The police telephoned the house. Wanting to find Connie. That's why I'm here."

The three Farley women had taken counsel and decided that Connie should not make herself available yet.

"Who is her lawyer?"

"I hope it doesn't come to that."

"What was your sister's reaction?"

"Well, you can imagine. Coming on top of the kidnapping. We are all at our wit's end." She studied the priest again. "And all you wanted to know was how I found out."

"Not all. Has there been a ransom demand for little Timothy?"

Her head dipped slightly and she looked sternly at him. "Father, Connie told us the stupid trick she pulled this morning."

"Ah. That is what I wanted to know. Your sister put me in a position where I either colluded in deception or exposed her to a very serious charge."

"Where is the baby?"

"Safe. What plan did the three of you come up with to show the kidnapping charge was just a mistake?"

"That's why I'm here. To pick up the

baby. My story will be that I took him from the car without telling Connie because I was worried to see him left alone and when I came back with the baby the car was gone and I couldn't locate her and . . ." Her voice trailed away. "I'll be more convincing when I tell the police."

"You'd do that for Connie?"

A tight little smile. "She's not heavy, she's my sister. We have been pulling Connie out of tight spots all her life."

"What did she tell you about her husband?"

"That she thought he meant to kidnap Timothy? In one way it's credible. On the other hand, it is the last thing he would do. Peter could not care for a baby without help."

"Did she say when she saw him last?"

"No. She took the news very badly. I suppose she feels some guilt, but finally she did love him, you know. She fought the divorce. She never believed they wouldn't be together again. Now that is beyond reach forever."

"Not forever."

"In this life, then."

"Connie visited Peter Rush's office in the Fenwick Mall this morning. She was seen leaving there at ten. The dry cleaning store is also in the Fenwick Mall."

"Did the police tell you that?"

He nodded. "Do you mind if I light this pipe?"

"Is it out?" She sniffed the fragrant air of the study. "Dad smoked a pipe."

He saw that she was trying to adjust to what he had just said. Next she would ask about all these wonderful books.

He said, "The police will want to know what she was doing there. We have to face the fact that her being at his office and his being found dead there will be put together."

Liz Farley was genuinely shocked. "Connie couldn't kill anyone. She couldn't have killed Peter if he were Jack the Ripper. She loved him."

He let the remark join the pipe smoke in the room. Liz must know that people are usually killed by husband or wife, a member of the family, a friend. The chances of being murdered by a stranger are slim indeed. The self-possessed woman who had entered his study bore little resemblance to the worried younger sister across his desk.

"Father, what are we going to do?"

"Who was your sister's lawyer in the divorce case?"

"Amos Cadbury. After the outcome of that, I don't think she will want him now."

"Who then?"

She inhaled, looked vaguely around, lifted her shoulders and dropped them. "It will have to be Mr. Cadbury. It wasn't his fault, it was that awful judge."

Father Dowling rose. "I'll come back to the house with you and we can discuss it together."

"But what of Timothy?"

"Believe me when I say he could not be in better hands. A wife and mother here in the parish, Mrs. Hospers, is looking after him. Do you know her?"

Liz nodded, all apprehension about her nephew gone.

"Did you bring a car?"

"I walked. Taking shortcuts." She looked sheepish. "In case I was followed."

"We can walk back, if you like."

Among the many attractions of St. Hilary's parish was that its streets were safe to walk at night. Roger Dowling told Marie where he was going and the housekeeper squeezed Liz's hand.

"Don't worry," she urged. "I said a prayer to St. Anthony. St. Anthony never fails."

Father Dowling wondered what Marie Murkin had specifically requested of St. Anthony of Padua.

—— Nine ——————————————

Say it in whispers, but Tuttle, of Tuttle & Tuttle, Attorneys at Law, had just turned fifty-nine. He could discern no sign of this in his mirror when he shaved of a morning. The reflected face looked the same to him as it had when he began to shave regularly at seventeen. But from time to time he would see himself in a plate-glass window as he hurried down a street, and that was no kid. Retirement? An indication of how ill-prepared Tuttle was for retirement was that he had begun to wonder if Social Security would still be solvent when he needed it.

Nonetheless, he liked to dream of retirement. Sitting in his office, feet on the desk, his Irish hat pulled low over his eyes, he would think of it. His enemies might have said he was already retired, and the truth was that business was bad. Tuttle had run a30-secondpost-midnight spot on a local channel and been kidded mercilessly at the courthouse for a week.

"It's ethical," he protested. "Check it out."

But it was the ad itself they made fun of. Tuttle in a three-piece suit, uncomfortable in the office set the TV studio had provided, phony books on a phony shelf, a desk no one had ever worked at. Tuttle sat on it, sort of sidesaddle, just one cheek touching, the idea being to look informal. His voice had sounded thin and unconvincing. Eager. Even Tuttle thought he looked in need of a lawyer himself. Still, it brought in a few clients and paid for itself.

Not that he was tempted to run it again. He could hustle up clients himself and rely on Peanuts and Old Tom. The prospect before him was to die with his boots on. On his desk. Retirement? Once he had been moved by those ads featuring the distinguished elderly couple, out in a boat, he fishing, she smiling into the camera. Retire to Florida. Sure. Tuttle had made a flying trip to St. Petersburg last winter to present some papers for the court, and the sight of all the oldsters on three-wheel bikes put an end to the dream for him. The whole damned place was like a hospital. And all the cases were terminal. No thanks. Give him the dirty old Fox River any day, and this office. A jug, a loaf and thou, as the poet says. Tuttle loved Shakespeare.

The law itself had been his main education. Tuttle senior, the other Tuttle in Tuttle & Tuttle, had not been a lawyer, but the son conferred an honorary degree on him in gratitude for helping him through law school and retaining confidence in him when the whole faculty seemed determined to flunk him out. One of his great regrets was that his father had not lived long enough to share the office and talk over cases with him. The panorama of human life. The joys and sorrows of mankind. Oh, it was mainly the seamy side he saw, of course. People go to law as a last resort. Trouble is a great leveler, the common denominator. The rich can afford more expensive counsel, they can buy one another off, but behind all that they have the same problems as anyone else.

Peanuts would listen when Tuttle waxed philosophical about his profession, but he never added anything to the conversation. Peanuts Pianone never added anything to any conversation. He would have been great in a Tarzan movie. As one of the apes. Tuttle laughed aloud, feeling bad about it. He liked Peanuts. Peanuts was his friend. But Old Tom was better to have around when a man wanted to have those long, long thoughts, as the poet says.

The scuttlebutt Peanuts brought about a reported kidnapping of the Rush kid set Tuttle thinking about the celebrated divorce case. Did Peanuts even remember it? The only thing Peanuts was sure to remember was who paid for the pizza last. So he rang up Old Tom, left a note with his sister or whoever it was answered, popped open a Diet Pepsi and tipped his hat over his eyes again. A boy's will is the wind's will, and the thoughts of youth—and of a fifty-nine-year-old, not too successful Fox River lawyer—are long, long thoughts.

He was still at it when Old Tom called and Tuttle told him to come on down.

"I'm at the courthouse," Tom said, a pleased lilt in his voice.

"Bring some cigars."

"What do you have to drink?"

"Pepsi."

"I'll bring a six-pack."

"Suit yourself."

Philosophy could thrive even on such creature comforts. Old Tom brought a bag of chips, too, and was pretty noisy chewing them. Besides, his dentures clacked, but it was nice nonetheless, having a kindred spirit there in the office.

"Where's your girl?" Tom asked.

"My girl?"

"Your secretary."

"This is her day off," Tuttle said. She had seven days a week off now, but there was no need to dwell on that. "Tom, I've been thinking of the Rush divorce."

"Funny."

"How so?"

"I have been too. Hear about the kidnapping?"

"Is that public?"

"I don't know."

Tuttle tipped up his hat. Old Tom wore a wise look. It would have been wiser if he had closed his mouth.

"The news is around the courthouse, huh?"

"Is that where you heard it?"

"Peanuts was in."

"I have other sources," Tom said.

This cat-and-mouse was not Tuttle's idea of a good session spent pondering the mystery of life.

"You got something you want to tell me?"

"Maybe."

Tuttle sailed his hat at the stand in the corner and made a perfect ringer. He got his shoes off the desk.

"I'm not going to beg, Tom."

He would have if he had known what Tom had seen. Tuttle cross-examined the old gent, and the story stood up, no imagining, no make-believe. Not even a man Tom's age could make up a story that complicated and keep it straight under cross-examination. Tuttle believed the story as if he himself had been a witness.

"Dowling, the priest, took the baby from the church to the rectory?"

"Why not? He finds a basket with a baby in it in his church."

"The way you said you saw him head for the church, Tom, he was going for that baby."

Tom frowned and swallowed, making his Adam's apple travel up and down his stalk of a throat.

"Don't you see, Tom? Someone told him the baby was there."

"Not me!"

"No, not you. Someone must have phoned him and said go look in the church."

"But who else knew?"

"Exactly. Mrs. Peter Rush called him. It had to be her."

"Tuttle, she never had time. There weren't five minutes went by after she left the baby and he went to the church."

"By God, you're right. Good thinking, Tom."

The Nobel Prize would be an anticlimax for Tom after such praise. He grinned so widely he nearly lost his upper denture.

"Tom, you wouldn't have a clothes basket at home, would you?"

"A clothes basket?"

"Like the one the baby was left in."

Tom said no and Tuttle might have dropped the thought, but when he was left alone it continued to tease him, one way in which he might put this information to profitable use. He could buy a clothes basket. The thought brought a frown. Maybe he would at that. Maybe he just would. He was sure he could convince her it was a good idea.

—— Ten ————————

Keegan stayed with it until he had a good preliminary picture of what had happened.

Time of death? Before noon, more precision to come. Weapon? The heavy glass ashtray with wickedly pointed corners found a few feet from the body, with plentiful evidence that it had been the means of toppling Peter Rush sideways to the floor with a mortal wound.

"He might have been saved if someone had gotten to him right after he was struck," Kunert said. "Of course there might have been brain damage, but he could have survived to live a normal life."

"The blow didn't kill him?"

"The bleeding did." Kunert spoke with the exactitude of a man who divides life into dozens of categories. Phil Keegan would bet Kunert had a personal computer at home with his personal finances, the books in his library, his fishing fly collection, his tools, everything—entered, numbered, classified.

"They're connected, aren't they?" Keegan said dryly.

Kunert gave it thought. "Temporally. One came before the other."

Keegan turned away. He could imagine what a defense lawyer would do with Kunert on the stand. He had seen too many smarties break down an action until you didn't know what you were talking about. Pulling the trigger. Odd things occurring in the chamber of the weapon. A projectile moving from point A to point B. Projectile entering human body. Vivid description of dermal, subdermal and internal damage caused by projectile. Harvey's theory of the circulation of the blood. Death certificate. Put them all together and they spell murder to any rational human being, mainly because no rational human being would think of all those as different acts or events. Who was the guy who said that motion is impossible because at any given moment the body is in a definite place and what is in a definite place is not moving? Nowadays he would be a defense lawyer. Or worse, a judge. Molly Jones.

The mobile lab had all but completed its work, picking up samples, photographing, the works. Agnes had found a lipstick wedged down between the cushions of the leather couch that stood along a wall at right angles to the desk.

"Unless Rush liked to make up when no one was looking, this could be important."

Keegan nodded. "And it could have been there for years."

"He was a make-out artist, not a makeup one," Cy said, seeming to surprise even himself. "That could belong to a woman who has nothing to do with this."

"It depends on how long it's been there," Keegan repeated.

"Look, is it all right if it's checked out?" Agnes did not like this cool reaction to her find. The lipstick was already in a plastic bag and set aside with other things destined for the lab.

"Of course it will be checked out. So what do you think happened here?"

Cy did the talking, which made for a quicker report. The papers on the desk were a mess, not as bad as those on the receptionist's desk in the outer office, but Rush, unlike Dr. Kunert, did not have tidy habits. Without someone to file his stuff, he just let it pile. There were the papers covering his divorce, insurance policies, various prospectuses for surefire get-rich schemes. A bank statement that looked like

Brazil's, all debts. And warning letters. Dunning letters. A notice from a collection service. Rush owed everyone. Keegan was reminded of the way his father had said thanks. Much obliged. Wasn't that Brazilian, too? *Obrigado.*

"What we have is a lot of people who would want him alive and well and able to pay those bills."

"Some lenders play rough. A man as desperate as Rush is a natural for sharks. There wouldn't be a lot of paper covering those transactions. And he miss a few payments, he dead." Agnes had slipped into the patois of the ghetto from which she had emerged. "Believe me, I've seen it happen. You make a lesson of the one who doesn't pay."

"Just speculation?" Keegan asked.

"So far. Should I check?"

Keegan nodded.

Agnes said, "He's been in my neighborhood. One of those banks is run by blacks. Maybe they were proud to add a white to their debtors. Of course they were charging him a very high interest. Which he wasn't paying."

"His wife was here," Cy said, taking it to where he knew it belonged. Was Agnes just being thorough or looking out for a sister? It had to be the former. Agnes would not care for Connie Farley.

"The girl across the hall saw her around ten o'clock. On the stairway you took to get here. Mrs. Rush going down, in a hurry, didn't even notice the woman, although she wasn't looking for a greeting."

"Looks bad," Keegan said.

"Or good, if we want to wrap this up."

"I thought you wanted to check out loan sharks, Agnes?"

"I do. This will be a good excuse. But it looks like she did it. She had motive."

"Motives," Cy corrected.

"You think all those debtors are out of it?"

Cy stood silently for a moment. Then he shook his head. "I say check out everything. She been found yet?"

Keegan did not know. He put in a call and got a negative answer. Keegan did not like that. She had reported a kidnapping at midday and had not been seen or heard from since. Had something happened to her as well? He could see that Cy and Agnes were wondering the same thing. Keegan dialed again and got the morgue.

"A beautiful woman, thirties? Naw." In person Sweeney looked dour enough for his job, but on the phone his voice gurgled like a comedian's. "You into fat middle-aged men, I got a couple of those."

"Keep your eye out," Keegan advised. "And my teeth in. Yes, sir."

It was after eleven when Keegan started back to St. Hilary's, late, but not too late for Roger Dowling. Keegan could not rid himself of the thought that Connie Farley had done another stupid thing after she conked her husband with the ashtray. To himself, he could admit this looked like an open-and-shut case. Connie and her husband had been quarreling for years, and the divorce suit she had contested made a public thing of her unhappy marriage. And then that judge awarding alimony to Rush! That would not have cleared up his debts, but it made the defeat twice as bitter. It wasn't hard to imagine what any conversation between those two would have been like this morning. Rush would not have been physically frightened of Connie, so she could easily get close enough to swing that ashtray without alarming him. Maybe she didn't know what she was going to do until she did it. From the divorce trial Keegan knew that she had threatened him with physical violence regularly but had never touched a hair of his head. Well, it only takes once. Rush would have gone over like a sack of flour. Then what? Panic, horror, remorse? Whatever, she beat it out of there.

Leave it to Father Dowling to find difficulties in this apparently open-and-shut case.

"The door of Peter Rush's office was locked, was it not?"

"When Cy tried it? Sure. It locks when you shut it."

A puff on the pipe. "But why assume Connie closed it? Why not assume that, like Lieutenant Horvath and Officer Lamb, she tried the door, found it locked and then, unlike them, left?"

Keegan smiled sarcastically. "Why think she even tried the door? Maybe she went halfway up the stairs, changed her mind and came down again, and that is when she was seen?"

Roger nodded, taking this quite seriously. "And there are many other possible explanations."

"Which her lawyer can dream up without our help. What would help is talking with Connie."

"I wondered if you had."

"She hasn't been found."

"Where have you looked?"

Keegan put down his beer but decided against asking Roger if he knew something he wasn't telling. Roger always knew something he wasn't telling. Oh, the hell with it.

"I just hope nothing has happened to her, Roger."

"How do you mean?"

"It happens. This kind of killing, more unintended than intended, the killer is filled with self-loathing and decides she doesn't deserve to live."

"Suicide?"

"As I say, it happens."

"To a Farley? I thought you knew the family."

It was odd how they thought of Connie as one of the Farleys even though she had been married to Peter Rush for years. But wasn't it just the family pride that made suicide a possibility?

Later, lying sleepless in the apartment that seemed less home to him than his office, Phil Keegan found it impossible to think of Connie as lying somewhere dead by her own hand. Not a Farley.

And where might a missing Farley be found if not at the family home?

—— Eleven ————————

Old Tom decided he had never agreed with the general courthouse view that Tuttle was a phony. Sure, Tuttle had received more than his share of warnings from the bar commission, but he was the victim of his own zeal, you might say, a lawyer who did not wait for business to come to him but took the bull by the tail and by God went out and beat the bushes for himself.

The image of Tuttle in his office, feet on the desk, hat pulled low over his eyes, warred with this portrait of the intrepid counselor, but why not take Tuttle's word, rather than his enemies', that what he was doing in this characteristic posture was thinking?

"Your beat thinking is done when you're unaware of it," Tuttle assured Tom. "Like when you're asleep. I know you've read that and I have too, but the difference between us, Tom, and I hope I'm not being out of line, is that I know it's true. I have put it to the test and I have returned to tell you that it works. What I try for is a state resembling sleep, but still conscious, and I let the old subconscious earn her keep."

"I know what you mean," Tom said.

That was a dangerous moment, when Tuttle looked at him as if he was going to laugh. If he had, that would have torn it, and the hell with his big scoop. Let somebody else figure out what was going on. But Tuttle did not laugh.

"I think you do know, Tom. I think you do. We are members of the same fraternity."

So Tom had gone on and told Tuttle what he had seen out there at St. Hilary's, and the reaction was better than he had hoped. Tuttle nearly fell off his chair getting his feet onto the floor. And they had gone through it again and again, as if he were giving testimony and Tuttle had to break it down. It was exhilarating. People who ran down Tuttle as a lawyer were damned fools, Tom decided. This man knew his stuff. By the time they were through, they had their ducks all in a row, fact following fact, a chronology.

"Too bad the girl isn't here," Tuttle said. "I could dictate a memo.

"I know shorthand."

"You do!"

Tom nodded. His dream after he retired from the railroad was to be a court reporter, but talk about a fraternity. He could not break into the magic circle. Not that he thought it was a waste of time to have learned shorthand. Sometimes, sitting in a courtroom, waiting to be asked to serve a paper or something, he would take down the proceedings in a shorthand pad, not on a machine like the court reporter used, though Tom had been broken in on that as well. He wanted to keep the edge on his skills, just in case. Well, this session with Tuttle more than justified all that work and study.

Tuttle talked and Tom got it down, what the lawyer called a Horarium of Events. They got it as close as they could to the exact minute. Surprising how much had happened in a very short span of time.

"Tom, the most interesting thing is what isn't on our list."

"How Dowling knew?"

Tuttle grinned at him. Fraternity brothers. "Who telephoned him at . . ." Tuttle consulted the horarium. Tom had typed it up on Tuttle's girl's machine, which was stiff as hell, as if it hadn't been used in months. ("We send out a lot of work.")

Then Tuttle went to get some photocopies made while Tom picked up the pizza the lawyer had phoned for. ("They're not delivering today, Tom.") But at the pizza parlor the clerk said the rule was cash in hand and no deliveries so far as Tuttle was concerned.

So Tuttle had a wedge of pizza in one hand when he studied the horarium and put the phone call Dowling must have received between 1:25 and 1:30.

"And it wasn't from Mrs. Rush."

"Tom, let's not rush into that. I give her five minutes, no, say four, from the time she leaves the church to the time Dowling comes out the door of the rectory. Could she have hit a phone during those four minutes?"

Tom held out for someone else as caller, unwilling to relinquish the suggestion that had nearly overwhelmed Tuttle before they started on the pizza. Four minutes was too short. She drove away, she would have to park, the conversation had to take some time. Tuttle was tired of a phone call they were just guessing had been made.

"Suppose there was a note in the basket."

Bingo. He had done it again.

85

"Wonderful," Tuttle cried. "If I wasn't full of pizza I'd suggest we celebrate with some Chinese food."

When they parted, the idea was that Tom would go back to St. Hilary's and keep his eyes open. It was unlikely that anything visible would show up there, but wars were won and lost on making the wrong guess and Tuttle was for playing it safe.

"I'll cover downtown, Tom."

But when Tom called Tuttle's office the following morning at nine-thirty, the phone rang and rang unanswered. He called Peanuts and Peanuts said no, he hadn't seen Tuttle yet. "It's early, Tom."

Tom called Tuttle's home number and was about to hang up after a dozen rings—he counted them—when an angry voice shouted hello.

"Tuttle, this is Tom."

"Do you know what time it is!"

"Ten-oh-five."

"Are you sure?"

Tom said he was sure. Tuttle said his watch had stopped. None of that mattered now that he had reached his partner.

"Peter Rush was killed yesterday in his office."

The whistle on the phone began as a

scarcely audible hiss and grew to ear-blasting shrillness.

"Where are you now, Tom?"

"Home. I've been trying to reach you."

"Meet me at my office in half an hour, will you? I'll get hold of Peanuts too."

Tom wasn't sure he liked that—he and Tuttle were doing pretty well without involving the runt of the Pianone litter. But it would have seemed petty in a Nobel Prize winner to cavil at something so small.

—— Twelve ——

The interval between Phil Keegan's two visits last night had been occupied by a conference at the Farley home, where Amos Cadbury made it all too understandable why Connie had done so badly contesting her husband's divorce suit.

"Is it official that Peter is dead?" Cadbury wanted to know.

"Are you doubting it?" Connie clearly found it difficult to be patient with Cadbury. Calling him had not been her idea.

"I like to stand on firm ground," Cadbury said.

Father Dowling said that he had it on

the authority of Captain Keegan. "And the police telephoned the Farleys."

"My very point. And Captain Keegan, too, was informed by telephone. We know what mischief can be accomplished by means of the telephone."

"I called the police and reported that Timothy had been kidnapped," Connie said. "Just accomplishing a little mischief, of course."

Cadbury turned to Mrs. Farley. "Is this true?"

"Yes, Amos, it is."

"And where is the child?"

Mrs. Farley put a hand over her mouth and looked at the lawyer with wide, embarrassed eyes.

"There's no need to worry about Timothy," Father Dowling said. "He is being taken care of by one of the parishioners."

Mrs. Farley looked from the priest to her daughter and back again. "You're not just saying that to ease my heart?"

Connie said, "Mr. Cadbury, I just wanted to get Timothy out of Peter's reach."

Cadbury's eyebrows had risen several notches during this revelation. Now he assumed a serious expression. "I would have preferred your not telling me."

"Does listening make you an accomplice?" Connie teased.

Cadbury looked at her coldly. "Not in murder, young lady, which is what you will most certainly be charged with in the morning. And that, I think you will agree, is no laughing matter. The caliber of the judiciary in these dark days is such that I no longer feel competent to predict what any judge might do. The law has become the plaything of imbeciles. I may not be the best one to represent you."

"Of course you are," Mrs. Farley cried. "You have been our lawyer as long as I can remember."

"That is part of the problem, dear lady. Nor has criminal law been my forte. I tell you quite frankly I have never defended in a murder case."

"Must we use that word?" Liz said, shivering.

"If we wish to discuss the facts." Cadbury turned to Roger Dowling. "Father, I am accepting your voucher that Peter Rush was murdered."

"I only pass on to you what the police told me, Mr. Cadbury. But I think you are right in saying that a charge will be brought against Connie."

"Of course it will," Connie said impatiently. "The important thing is that I did not do it."

"If only your word were sufficient," Cadbury said dryly. It was obvious to Father Dowling that the lawyer had less than a flattering view of his client. What a pair they made, Connie and Amos Cadbury. "Here is what we are going to do. You will spend the night in a motel and in the morning . . ."

"A motel!"

"I am surprised the police haven't come here with a search warrant already. They may come at any time. I do not want you to be arrested. In the morning, we shall all—your mother, your sister and I—appear at police headquarters. You will volunteer to be all the help you can in this terrible matter. We must put on a bold face, making it as close to impossible as we can for the police to accuse you."

"I cannot sleep in motels," Connie complained.

"Good. We shall be up for most of the night in any case. I want to know what you have been up to during this day and in any preceding days which cast light on this one. You must confide in me utterly. If that is

90

too distasteful a prospect, then I give you another chance to seek counsel elsewhere."

Connie made a face. "You're my lawyer."

"Very well. Pack a few things and we will be off."

"Where are you going?" Liz asked.

"I must not tell you. When asked, you can honestly say you do not know. Where is the telephone?"

Cadbury had been transformed. His phone conversation was quite audible. He told his secretary that he would be stopping by for her in fifteen minutes. Roger Dowling felt better about Connie's chances than he had at the outset. Cadbury returned to the living room.

"I want the baby who was erroneously reported kidnapped to be with us in the morning."

"I'll get him," Liz said.

That settled, Cadbury ordered Mrs. Farley to get a good night's sleep. A sardonic laugh escaped her.

"If only it were that easy."

"Take a pill."

"I hate pills."

"Then don't complain. At our age, taking pills is the price we pay to keep going. I myself will take a pill in order to stay awake."

"I may need one myself," Connie said.

"The prospect of hanging wonderfully concentrates the mind. Dr. Johnson. Of course he was speaking only of males."

Roger Dowling wondered if the lawyer was troubled by thoughts of Judge Molly Jones.

Walking back to the rectory, the air balmy, the night sky very remote despite the friendly twinkling of the stars, Roger Dowling let his mind roam. Morning star. Star of the sea. All those lovely titles applied to the mother of Jesus. A stable reference in a wheeling world. "O, no, it is an ever-fixèd mark/That looks on tempests and is never shaken." Love. The lines occurred in Shakespeare's sonnet that begins: "Let me not to the marriage of true minds/Admit impediments." Well, impediments enough had been admitted into the Rush marriage, and now Peter was dead and his divorced wife in danger of being accused of the crime.

—— Thirteen ————————

At three in the morning Keegan called Cy Horvath, waking him and his wife from a slumber all the deeper because they had bowled four lines when Cy finally got home the night before.

"She's got to be at the Farley house, Cy. Get Jensen to issue a bench warrant and go out there and arrest Connie Farley."

"You mean Connie Rush."

"Would we have held off like this if I didn't know the family?"

Cy had turned away from the phone to enjoy a yawn that squeezed his eyes shut and cut off his hearing.

"You know we wouldn't," Keegan said, answering his own question.

"You think she's at her mother's house?"

"She's got to be. Elimination."

"You're calling her mother a liar."

"It's not lying when you're trying to help your kids."

"Why don't I check her place again before bothering the old lady?"

"I already did. No answer. There's no one there. The building manager hadn't seen her all day."

"You woke him up?"

"He was happy to help."

Cy wished he felt the same. Say Mrs. Rush was holed up at her mother's, waiting a couple hours wouldn't change anything.

Cy had decided that the previous afternoon she was more than likely at the Farley house. In a way it was nice. If she thought she had them fooled, she would stay put and be there when they needed her. More and more, she looked like the one.

Jensen signed the warrant without coming fully awake. Agnes had said she wanted in when Cy called her, so he swung past her place and they headed for the Farley house.

"Keegan can't sleep, nobody sleeps, is that it?"

"He couldn't sleep because he thinks we've been playing favorites."

Agnes nodded, reconciled with this early-morning duty.

They stood on the Farley doorstep at four in the morning, warrant in hand, ready to take Constance Farley Rush into custody as a material witness to her husband's murder. Only she wasn't there.

Elizabeth Farley, her gray hair in a ponytail, wearing a robe that was several shades of green, assured them her sister was not in the house.

"When did she leave?"

Miss Farley might not have looked completely awake but she was. She gave Agnes a little smile.

"The point of this warrant is that we can come in and look."

"At this hour?"

"As long as we're all up, it seems as good a time as any."

"I can't believe you have that right."

"If you would like to call your lawyer, go right ahead. We will just stand here freezing on your doorstep."

There were two patrol cars on watch in case Connie tried to slip away while they were delayed at the door. But Miss Farley stepped aside and let them in.

"All right, let's get it over with. Do we have to wake my mother?"

But Mrs. Farley was coming downstairs as they entered, her white hair braided, her eyes rimmed with pink.

"Police, Mrs. Farley."

"Police? Of course. Anything is possible now. As Mr. Cadbury says. Storm troopers in the night."

Agnes said, "We spoke yesterday, Mrs. Farley."

"I know. When you came looking for my daughter. What is it this time?"

"The same thing, ma'am. We have single-track minds and we just can't shake the thought that your daughter is here. In fact, we were ordered to come here with the search warrant that Lieutenant Horvath is holding."

"You want to search the house?"

"Mother, let them. The sooner they start, the sooner it will be over."

Cy decided right there that they were on a wild-goose chase. There was something feigned in the indignation of the two women. Not that they weren't really annoyed to be awakened this early. But Cy had the same feeling he had had as a kid when they were playing hide-and-seek and he was being urged down a false path. Liz and her mother were too willing to have the house searched for it to be a fruitful deed. But he hadn't been sent here to make psychic guesses about Mrs. Farley and her daughter.

"You take upstairs," he said to Agnes. Cy didn't want to be poking around in their bedrooms, particularly when he didn't expect to find anything, and Agnes apparently had the same thought. He made a perfunctory sweep of the downstairs, the basement, the garage, and when he came inside, Agnes had finished upstairs.

"The bird has flown," she announced to Cy. "The question is where."

"We don't know," Mrs. Farley said firmly, her first misstep.

"When did she go?"

Liz said, "You came here looking for my sister. You now know she is not here. Doesn't that exhaust the authority of your warrant?"

"Almost," Cy said. "You deny knowing where your sister is?"

"Categorically."

Again Cy saw something in her eye. The glint a person gets when he thinks he can tell a lie by telling the truth and is thereby home free.

"Thank you for your cooperation."

"What next?" Agnes asked when they were back in the car.

"How about the Waffle House?"

"Which one of us will be Little Black Sambo?"

Touchy, touchy. He decided not to answer. Maybe if there were Hungarian jokes, he would know what made her feel that way.

—— Fourteen ——

The frantic call from Liz Farley came just minutes before Roger Dowling saw Edna Hospers pull into her accustomed place by the school and go with purposeful strides to the door, acknowledging the greetings of the oldsters, who, no matter how early she got there, always awaited her on the steps. This morning they were all the more eager because of her absence the previous day. Edna's arrival told Roger Dowling that something very wrong indeed had happened, and that he was implicated, all because of the silly scheme of Connie Farley Rush, who was at this very moment berating him on the telephone.

"You told me she was safe, Father Dowling. I trusted you."

"You certainly pressed me into your service. I'll talk with Mrs. Hospers and see what happened."

Liz came on again. "They are actually indicting her, Father."

"Surely they won't hold her."

"I don't know."

"Don't worry, they won't." He felt justified in giving this assurance; Phil Keegan was not likely to think that Connie Farley was going to leave the country. As it happened, he reckoned without Judge Jones, whose mission in life seemed to be to make things difficult for Constance Farley Rush. But Roger Dowling was not to know this until later. The imperative now was to bring this emotional phone call to an end and get over to the school to talk with Edna.

She was in the game room surrounded by her charges and smiled over their heads at Father Dowling when he caught her attention. She came toward him, in stages, shedding admirers on the way. Father Dowling had moved into the hallway.

"Do you have another baby for me, Father? What a darling he was."

"Someone picked him up?"

"Yes." She looked at him more closely. "Is something wrong?"

"Who came for the child?"

"A woman . . ." She grasped his arm. "Wasn't she the aunt?"

Beyond Edna, Father Dowling could see the uneasy expressions on some old people who had followed Mrs. Hospers to the door. "Let's go to your office."

In the office, Edna told him in frantic tones that, as arranged, a woman had come for the baby that morning and she had turned it over.

"She said, 'I've come for the baby,' and I handed him over. Of course. I'd been expecting her. Father, I feel like such a fool."

"Don't, Edna. If you'd asked who she was, she would have said Mrs. Rush and you would have gone ahead, wouldn't you?"

"She just took the basket and left. I felt like a hired babysitter or something. She didn't look at the baby, make a fuss, nothing like that. I should have known something was wrong, but I was relieved to turn him over. A baby that young! It's been such a long time. But who was the woman?"

Edna's description meant nothing to Father Dowling. Nor did it ring a bell with Liz Farley when he called her. Once more, Connie came on, calmer, but treating Roger Dowling somewhat as she had Amos Cadbury the night before.

"I have notified the police," she said coldly.

"Again?" He couldn't resist it, purgatory

or not. He knew his Dante and Aquinas well enough to know that it is just such petty deeds that separate us most, if not most seriously, from God. Connie was rendered momentarily silent.

"Yesterday they believed me," she said, subdued. "Now they think I'm a real yo-yo. Dear God, Father, what have I done? I'm being punished!"

For what? He did not ask, feeling contrite himself.

"I'll tell Captain Keegan the whole story."

"Don't expect much sympathy from him."

"I won't. Make them find my baby, Father Dowling."

What a mercurial woman she was, imperious and pitiable in the space of minutes. But her husband was dead and her baby was really missing now. Whether or not she was being punished he could not say, but she was certainly being tested.

And then, ready to be tested himself, he telephoned Phil Keegan.

"Are you coming to the noon Mass, Phil?"

"I'll try. Things are jumping."

"Come to lunch afterward."

"I'll have to eat and run."

"There's something I want to tell you."

"Sure you do. You mean you want to be filled in on the Connie Farley Rush matter."

"That too."

His Mass at noon was the focal point of Roger Dowling's day, the memorial of the sacrifice that had redeemed mankind from sin. It was his essential function as a priest to be a conduit through which the grace of God might come to men. As he stood at the altar, he was one with those huddled figures in catacombs, with missionaries who had moved out through barbarous Europe, bringing the faith and the Mass, with celebrants at massive Romanesque altars, with others in aspiring Gothic cathedrals, with chaplains on battlefields, with those on crusade and, on this very day, with others of his order all around the globe. At every point on the clock, somewhere this sacrifice was being reenacted to remind the faithful what had been done for them. Looking out at the several dozen regulars at the daily Mass, Roger Dowling felt united with them and with all the priests and faithful of today and back through the centuries to the catacombs of Santa Constarza on the Via Nomentana in Rome.

Phil Keegan was not in the church.

But he was at the rectory when Father Dowling returned, Phil's huge figure seeming to fill half the kitchen as he talked with Marie. The housekeeper's mouth was a thin line. She might have locked it and thrown away the key. Keegan seemed relieved to see the priest.

"Before you start feeding me, I have to ask about a crazy story Connie Rush has been telling."

"I will tell you all I know while we eat. Come into the dining room."

After a ruminative grace, Roger Dowling said, "Phil, I have not been frank with you these past days."

"No! I can't believe it."

"I knew something you wanted to know and had a right to know, and I did not tell you. In extenuation, I could say that I was in that condition St. Thomas calls perplexity. No matter what I did, it seemed I must do something wrong."

"Damned if you do, damned if you don't?"

"I hope the stakes are not so stark. But that is the general idea. Connie more or less forced me into a position where I was colluding with her attempt to make the police think her child had been kidnapped."

"She said she left it in the church."

"And so she did. I received a call telling me the baby was there. It was. In a basket. I brought it here."

Keegan sat back and laughed. "I would have liked to see that. The pastor carrying a baby into the rectory."

"It does have Boccaccio-like possibilities."

Keegan frowned, and Father Dowling did not explain. Phil would be no less a man for not knowing Boccaccio.

"Marie could not take care of an infant . . ."

"I could! But only if I dropped everything else. It was such a tiny thing. Besides, I can't manage two babies."

He ignored that. "I asked Edna Hospers to look after it, and she did, taking the baby home."

"I'll be damned."

"I profoundly hope not. That is half the story. The ruse. Now comes dramatic irony. This morning the baby was to be picked up and to form part of the Farley party that Cadbury led to your office. The baby was picked up, all right, but before Liz Farley came for it. Liz was told by Edna's children the baby was gone. Phil, this time the baby is genuinely missing."

Although he listened attentively to the pastor, Phil's consumption of Marie's *risotto con piselli e funghi* went on apace.

"Kidnapped?"

"As far as I know, there has been no ransom demand. Taking a baby against its will? How else is a child to get around? Against the will of the mother, yes. If that is kidnapping, this is a kidnapping."

"We'll call it kidnapping," Phil said impatiently. "And impersonating the mother."

"Apparently the woman said nothing much at all to Edna. She said she had come for the baby. And she took it."

"Well, Roger, this is certainly not Connie's day. She was arraigned before Judge Molly Jones, who has taken under advisement the request that bail be set. Cadbury nearly blew a fuse, though you would have to know him to realize it. The worse Judge Jones gets, the more elaborately chivalrous he becomes. That drives her wild. If he keeps it up, Connie will end up doing life without coming to trial."

Roger Dowling sighed. "It is a great relief to tell you all this."

"Confession is good for the soul."

"It is indeed." And Roger Dowling bent to his *risotto* with a gusto he had not felt when it was put before him.

"Let me get you some warm," Marie said.

"This is ambrosia, Marie. It is perfect."

Phil was not gone an hour when Cy Horvath and Agnes Lamb came to talk to Edna. Afterward, they stopped at the rectory.

"The Farleys can't guess who the woman was," Cy told Father Dowling. "Chances are they are the only ones who will know."

Connie had been asked to make a list of women who were in any way like the person Edna had described, but she had not known where to begin. "Friends, enemies, relatives," Keegan suggested, but that had not helped. A name was written and almost immediately scratched out. Finally, she had crumpled up the sheet. "I just don't know." Liz Farley had been of no more help. The names she had given them were of women who had once served as babysitters for the Farleys when she and

Connie were children. But they were as old as Mrs. Farley now. She had also mentioned an *au pair,* present whereabouts unknown: Bridget Connor. Or was it O'Connor? The sisters tried to remember and Cy gave up on them. Of course it was possible they really had no idea who had picked up little Timothy Rush.

"I wonder who would be asked for ransom?" the priest said.

"Were you really involved in this, or is Mrs. Rush giving us a story?"

"Lieutenant, I went to the church when someone phoned to say a baby in a basket would be found in a back pew. Once I brought the baby here, I was in it."

"Nice lady," Agnes said.

"Edna Hospers is pretty upset," Cy said.

"She thinks she did something wrong. She did not. But fine distinctions about responsibility don't always help."

"This is quite a library, Father," Agnes said. "Books, pipe smoke, coffeepot simmering. Nice. Have you read all these books?"

"'Read' is an analogous term."

"I'm sorry I asked."

After they left, Father Dowling thought of the implications of Agnes's remark. The clerical life must look comfortable. Because it was. In recent years, many men had left the priesthood, applying for and receiving laicization, and many of them grumbled about what a repressed life they had lived as clerics. Roger Dowling suspected that Agnes Lamb's estimate was closer to the truth. Not that it was all sitting around, smoking a pipe and reading. There were even more satisfying aspects of the life. Saying Mass, dispensing the sacraments, representing the ways of God to man. If a priest kept alert to what he was doing—and that required prayer—it was a profoundly satisfying life.

—— Fifteen ——————————

Tuttle did not believe it.

He had put Old Tom on the lookout at St. Hilary's largely to keep him out of the way. He had decided on a use for the information that had come to him, and he did not mean to tip his hand to anyone, not to Tom, not to Peanuts. To his father, God rest his soul, if he were alive, perhaps, but to no one else.

Besides, he was covering his rear. He did

not expect a warm welcome when he approached Amos Cadbury; with a starchy bastard like that, anything might happen. He had not forgotten that Cadbury had been a member of a committee that voted to censure him. But Tuttle for one was willing to let bygones be bygones. Cadbury's interest was his client, and he would leave no stone unturned to defend her. The image was vaguely unsettling. What emerged when one turned over a rock was not the way he wished to think of this case just now. He preferred to view the offer he was about to make as a professional gesture, one lawyer helping another. For a fee, needless to say.

Tuttle had kept abreast of the Rush divorce in a variety of ways. Courthouse scuttlebutt, a long evening spent drinking with Mervel, who covered the proceedings for the Fox River *Tribune*, Old Tom; and several times he had taken a pew in Judge Jones's court and watched. Talk about your human comedy.

Courtrooms are places where, within limits and according to the rules of evidence, relevance and the like, one can let it all hang out, and the Rushes seemed determined to get at one another in public. If her lawyer tried to stanch the flow, he goaded his client on, and Judge Molly Jones—who had to be the most unusual occupant of the bench in Tuttle's career—seemed to make up the rules as she went along. Cadbury had tried to right things later, filing papers like crazy, in order to get a higher court to review what Jones had done. How in hell had such a woman become a judge? It was no mystery to Peanuts, whose relatives in City Hall had backed her for the vacancy.

"Because she's a broad."

"There are lots of broads."

Peanuts shrugged. The higher reaches of logic did not interest him.

What had interested Tuttle philosophically, as he was not ashamed to say to Mervel and Tom, was Constance Farley Rush. Judge Jones could be explained almost as simply as Peanuts suggested. Explaining a real woman like Constance Farley Rush was another matter.

Mervel, who had been off the sauce for three weeks but had repented, was pretty sloshed the night he and Tuttle discussed Constance Rush.

"Simple," Mervel said. "A woman scorned."

He was as bad as Peanuts. "Then why didn't she sue *him* rather than let him haul her into court?"

"She's Catholic."

"You got any two-word reasons?"

Mervel smiled. "Not when one's enough. She's Catholic."

"So is her husband. So am I. What's that got to do with it?"

"I didn't know you were Catholic."

"I don't like to parade my religious faith," Tuttle said loftily. It had been seven years since he had seen the inside of a church. "You been paying attention, Mervel, you would have noticed Catholics getting divorced like everybody else now. Before or after they get an annulment. It's a new world."

"Not for someone like Constance Farley."

"Farley Rush."

"What I'm thinking about has more to do with her family. She *is* a Farley, Tuttle. Don't you know what that means in Fox River?"

Did he know what it meant? But Tuttle held his anger in check. This was more like the conversation he wanted. Tuttle knew that beneath the booze and cynicism

111

there lurked a philosopher in his reporter friend. Mervel remarked that he had heard it said she was throwing mud at her family name.

"Bullshit, if you'll excuse the expression. That is herself she is hurting in that courtroom, not her family. Her father's dead—and he was something—her mother is almost gaga, and her sister takes care of Mom. She's like a nun in sheep's clothing."

"Huh?"

"Think about it."

"Tell me."

"It's all the Catholic thing. The Fourth Commandment."

"Refresh my memory."

"Honor thy father and mother."

Tuttle liked this. If he could lay claim to any virtue, it was piety. He had genuinely loved his father, and to this day he tried to act in such a way that his father would approve. Some men have consciences. Tuttle had his father. Now he knew why he was fascinated by Constance Farley Rush. They were kindred spirits. What she was doing was tied up with her father. He didn't know how, but he was sure of it. Thereby she commanded his respect, and from that point of view woe betide the sonofabitch who made a crack about her in Tuttle's presence. He even drafted a letter to Cadbury after Judge Jones's ruling. He would have sent it too, if he had had a secretary to type it up.

"There is an element of confessing one's sins and doing public penance."

"I think she wants to hurt her husband too, Mervel."

"Yes." Mervel squinted through the smoke of his cigarette. "But he's her, too. Two in one flesh. Marriage as sacrament. Oh, it all hangs together, Tuttle."

Mervel was right. Tuttle told him so. He told him there weren't two reporters in a hundred who could see what Mervel saw. He congratulated him and fixed him another drink, the one that put him away for the night, which he spent on Tuttle's couch.

When Tom came to him with his incredible story, Tuttle had somehow seen that it too fitted in. How? There was something biblical in it, but he had been raised a Catholic and the Bible had come to him only in bits and pieces, as Epistles and Gospels at Mass. Moses? Something like that.

Whatever it was, he doubted Connie had confided in Cadbury, and who could blame her? Cadbury's manner suggested that he was consigned to walk the earth awhile for his sins, rubbing elbows with mere mortals. He was going to be a hard guy to help, but Tuttle had made up his mind. He drafted another letter and this one he typed and sent, using Mervel's machine in the pressroom at the courthouse. He told Mr. Cadbury that he was in possession of information vitally important to his client Mrs. Rush, and he would be happy to discuss it with fellow counsel at the earliest mutually convenient time. Cordially, B. F. Tuttle, LL.B.

When the phone rang, he got poised before answering, thinking it must be Cadbury.

"I'll get it, Miss Hudson," he called over his shoulder as he picked up the receiver. "Tuttle here."

But it was Old Tom with the news that another baby had been left in St. Hilary's church.

"Not another one," Tom corrected. "The same one."

"You're pulling my leg."

"This time Dowling saw me see him, couldn't help that, I knew you would want a full report."

"Did you see who left it?"

"No."

"Was it left in a clothes basket?"

"That's right. What in hell is going on, Tuttle?"

"Tom, if you're confused, how do you think Dowling feels?"

But Tuttle was not confused. Surprised, but not confused. He had left the basket with her despite the fact that she said the idea was a crazy one. But why had she put the baby in the church again?

—— Sixteen ———————

"The baby's back," Keegan said to Cy, holding his hand over the phone. He removed it. "Who you giving it to this time?"

"Well," Roger Dowling said. "I called you."

"I understand that. So what do we have? A mislaid baby no longer mislaid. What crime has been committed?"

"Phil, I feel bad enough for keeping it from you the first time."

Keegan did not like to act righteous with Roger Dowling; they were too good friends for that. Dowling got him mad as hell many times, but in the end Keegan knew his life would be much emptier if he couldn't shoot the bull with the pastor of St. Hilary's one or two nights a week. What bothered him was that this repetition suggested that Roger had staged the second event to make up for the first.

"But that doesn't make sense," Agnes said after he had hung up and voiced this possibility. "Chances are he's a little tired of finding babies in his church."

"Baby," said Cy. "It's the same one."

Keegan almost resented the two of them presuming to tell him how Roger Dowling felt.

"Did Judge Jones set bail for Mrs. Rush yet?"

"Half an hour ago. But Molly had a statement for the press, too, explaining that this was not special treatment because of Mrs. Rush's wealth and social standing."

"Well, now she's got her baby back and we aren't making much progress on the murder of her husband. I don't want it said we are showing favor because of her wealth and social standing."

Wealth. He supposed the term fitted. But the surprise he felt on hearing it applied to Connie Farley lingered. These events had the effect of bringing back an earlier time at St. Hilary's.

"Tell me about it," Roger said at lunch when Keegan mentioned this.

"Marie could tell you as much as I could."

"Do any two people have the same memories?"

"Of the Farleys?"

Marie Murkin sighed aloud. "Pillars of the parish, they always were. Look at Mrs. Farley, still at her age practically a daily communicant. Been that way most of her life, even when the girls were little."

"Was her husband the same?"

"Not many men have time for daily Mass, Father."

"But Sundays?"

"Oh my, yes. He was chief usher for years. What a fine figure of a man he was, taking up the collection, making sure people approached the communion rail in orderly fashion, a pew at a time. Mrs. Farley and the girls would be in a front pew, on the Blessed Virgin's side, but Mr. Farley was always in back. As an usher."

What vivid memories Marie's talking brought on. Phil Keegan could see old Farley moving majestically up and down the center aisle—never a side aisle: he was the chief usher. Phil himself preferred being with his wife and girls. That was another thing, his girls and the Farley girls. There had always been a friendly rivalry between them, at the parish school and later at St. Margaret's Academy. And he remembered the question his daughter Susan had once asked.

"Why doesn't Mr. Farley ever receive communion, Daddy?"

"Doesn't he receive every Sunday?"

Susan shook her head. "He never goes."

"Well, let's not pry into something like that, Susan. Anyway, I'm sure you're wrong."

Farley could have come to an earlier Mass, received communion and then had his breakfast before coming back to usher at the ten o'clock Mass. But he certainly did not receive communion at the ten. Despite himself, Keegan kept an eye on Farley and found that Susan was right. He never acknowledged it, of course. It was too private a matter. The explanation that teased the mind was the simplest: Farley did not receive communion because he could not. The impediment of mortal sin. Not being in the state of grace. So why not go to confession? In order to receive absolution, a person had to express a sincere resolve to avoid serious sin in the future.

Sitting at the rectory table, listening to Marie extol the Farleys, and Mr. Farley particularly, Keegan thought again of the old speculation that had begun unbidden because of his daughter's question, and continued despite his efforts to stop it. He had no right to speculate about the condition of another man's soul. Not even now when he was dead. Especially now. Roger had a Latin phrase for it, but Latin was the reason Phil Keegan had not stayed in the minor seminary where he had first known Roger.

Warring with the desire to think only well of the dead was his lifetime as a cop. He could not stop himself from thinking of the elegant usher of yesteryear, directing communicants down the aisle but never himself approaching the railing.

"You seem pensive, Phil."

"It is strange to think of old times in this parish."

"It has fallen on evil days?"

"Different days. And that's not your fault."

"Well."

"What I mean is that the whole neighborhood has changed. How many people like the Farleys stayed put when the Interstate was cut through? I moved myself."

"To get away from the noise?"

Roger said it gently. The priest knew him better than he thought. But the loss of his wife was a special reason. Others had left because the value of property began to sink and they wanted to cut their losses. All those beautiful big houses, family houses, abandoned. For a while it seemed the neighborhood, and the parish with it, would go completely to hell. But a change had set in. Younger couples were buying here now, attracted by the elegance and the solid construction as well as the prices of the houses.

—— Seventeen ——

The first time Mr. Farley told her she reminded him of a Murillo, she thought he meant a cigar, but from the very beginning she had sense enough to keep her mouth shut when she didn't understand him. He could read her silence anyway he wanted, and he saw something in her she herself did not recognize, though over the years the gap between her real self and the girl he imagined lessened. She learned a lot.

It began when she was hired as a file clerk in his office; not by him, but by Phibbs, the office manager. When she was introduced to the man himself, it was pretty much a formality until he really looked at her. From that moment things changed. He looked at her as if he had known her forever.

She would have had to be pretty dumb not to notice the way he continued to keep an eye on her, calling her into his office, always finding excuses to talk with her. Phibbs frowned but said nothing. It was Mr. Farley's practice to have tea in the afternoon. ("When?" she asked Phibbs. "At teatime, my dear.") She was given the job of making and serving his tea, taking over from the girl with half a year's seniority, who was delighted to be relieved of it.

"He's so fussy how it's made."

"I almost never drink tea. Iced tea sometimes, in the summer."

"My God, don't tell him that. And never, never mention tea bags. They are an abomination."

The girl was trying to imitate Mr. Farley,

not too badly either, but June was more nervous than amused. As it turned out, the tea ceremony was not all that bad. Mr. Farley told her exactly what to do, he was a natural teacher, and before long she looked forward to teatime as a break from the dullness of filing. It was during teatime that it began.

Nothing out of the way, of course; he was a perfect gentleman always. That was why she felt so comfortable with him. She did not know another soul like him, but he made her feel at ease. She was twenty-one and he was older than her father would have been if he had not been killed in Korea, but soon she felt more relaxed with Mr. Farley than with anyone else.

Their conversations were the oddest mixture of lecture and quiz. He wanted to know all about her, and he could get her to say things she had told no one else. But most of the time he was telling her things, educating her.

"You have a good mind," he said. "You shouldn't waste it."

He kept returning to this, telling her it was not too late, she should go to the university.

"I have to work."

"I could help you. I would grant you a Farley scholarship."

"First I'd have to finish high school."

She had dropped out and gone to business school, while she worked as a waitress in order to afford it. Working for Mr. Farley was a result of that effort to improve herself, and she didn't much like his suggestion that she should make something of herself. She already had and it had not been easy. But filing certainly was dull.

Phibbs began interrupting Mr. Farley more and more during teatime, obviously not liking the most junior person in the office chatting with the boss for nearly half an hour every afternoon. It was Phibbs who first made her think something else was going on, not that the office manager said anything, but his manner suggested he was breaking in on something when he came in. Mr. Farley shared a little smile with her.

"Phibbs doesn't understand," he said.

June said nothing. What could she say? She didn't understand either.

"You are becoming a third daughter to me."

There are remarks which, made by any other man his age to a young female employee, would make you laugh, but when he spoke it was like another ceremony, one of adoption. He would be the father she no longer had. And such a distinguished man, always immaculate, always even-tempered, and very, very shrewd.

"I cannot have my daughter working in the office. We must make other arrangements."

He meant it. He got her another job, helped her find an apartment in Evanston. She would get her high school diploma at night and then enter Northwestern, that had been the plan. He helped her furnish the apartment and it was beautiful, far more than she could afford, but of course he was paying for it.

It was so difficult to explain how easily it had all become something else. Taken in outline, there was no way it didn't sound like a middle-aged man setting up a girl as his mistress. But that is not the way she thought of it and she knew he didn't either. He had embarked on an exercise in self-deception that would occupy him until the day he died. But that had been his description, so he really had not deceived himself. He wanted to do what they did and at the same time not be doing it. He wanted to be everything he seemed, and was, and to have her as well. None of this was clear when she was first installed in the apartment. He made a final inspection and said goodbye. He took her hand and then—this seemed a ceremony, too—he kissed her solemnly on the cheek. "My daughter," he breathed.

He did not speak of the office when he came, and much of her own life was closed to him. But it was understood that her deepest emotional commitment was to him. He never asked questions, never quizzed her to find out whom she might be going out with. The truth was that he had spoiled her for younger men. Those her own age seemed impossibly crude and ignorant by comparison with him.

First, there was music. On each visit, he would bring a new record or album and they would listen to it. He would comment, explain, tell her stories about the composer and his mistresses, in such a way that it seemed part of the score. He brought her books. Books, books, books. She still had them all. But because the music came first, it made the deepest impression on her. What torture it was now to sit all day in Dunn's office, unable to shut out the Muzak that filled the mall like a plague.

The farewell kiss on the cheek came to include an embrace as well. He kissed her forehead, her chin, playfully, but with dignity too. And one night she lifted her mouth to his and it became what it was meant to be all along. She was not a virgin at the time, but there had only been one boy, in high school, years before. All manner, his long hair swept back, a swagger and side-of-the-mouth talk but quick as a bunny when it came to making out. Big deal. In one sense, then, she came to Mr. Farley a virgin.

It was like a dream when he made love to her. There was no haste, no frantic struggle. First there was a special bottle of wine, and music. A ceremony. Had he selected the bedroom lamps with an eye to this? She lay on satin sheets bathed in the rose glow of the lamps. Now when he mentioned Murillo, she knew what he meant. She felt like a mythological figure in a seventeenth-century painting, or a mortal maiden being taken by a god. She had admired Mr. Farley before, she had respected him, liked him, preferred his company to that of anyone else. Now she loved him.

And when it was over, she got her first inkling of what his religion meant to him. He was Catholic through and through. It came out in his discussion of painting and in the reading he had her do. Once she was settled in the apartment, he had decided that he would be her teacher; formal education was a waste of her time. After the first time he made love to her, he could not conceal that he was troubled. She listened as always. They had sinned seriously. He had no right to take her like this. She should be able to look forward to a husband and family. He went on, describing what they both knew she would never have and never want. She wanted him.

"I would be your husband if I could."

"You are."

An inspiration. Over the years he developed a theory about them. They simply did not fit the usual categories. To an outsider, theirs would seem to be an arrangement of convenience or a sordid affair. That was false. Not that any outsider had occasion to form an opinion. The Phibbses of this world were a thing of the past once she left the office. The building manager had the I.Q. you would expect. He thought Mr. Farley was her father, and no one else in the building saw him come or go. He parked in a municipal garage, telephoned and June let him into the garage. One flight up and they were in her apartment. Never once in all those years had anyone witnessed his arrival. She would drive him downtown to his car, and he would go home to his family in Fox River.

He called her his daughter, but it was some time before he told her of his family. When he did, it was clear that his theory about June enabled him to love his wife no less than he had. He was, he said, "a little world made cunningly," able to love two women, able to love his family, able to love her as well.

"Not that I presume to alter Church law in my favor."

He meant that he no longer received communion when he went to Mass. Catholicism was one of the things he instructed her in. One day she went inside a Catholic church and found that it did not frighten or repel her as it would have before Mr. Farley. He actually wanted her to become a Catholic. But later.

"Make me chaste, Lord, but not yet." She knew that was St. Augustine. Mr. Farley derived consolation from Augustine's difficulties with women. And Paul Claudel's. "After his famous conversion in Notre Dame, several years passed before he confessed."

The plan that emerged was this. They would go on as they were, but a time would come—he had turned fifty when they had this conversation—when their relationship would move to a higher plane. Pure friendship. He meant they would stop making love. She did not like that prospect, instinctively knowing that his attraction to her was far more sexual than he could admit. If he stopped making love to her, she feared they would stop seeing one another.

But in the plan he developed, a time would come when they would really be father and daughter. She could meet his family. Everything would be just as it should be. He could receive communion again, after he confessed his sins. She was included in his sins. She was the biggest sin of all. Eventually she would become a Catholic too. There was no point in it now, since they would continue to have one another, and whatever his theory about being an exemption to divine law, he felt bound by the laws of his Church.

She did not find any of this at all strange.

It heightened their relationship and raised it to the level of drama. They were different, she and Mr. Farley, they were like the lovers of literature, destined for one another but somehow prevented from having their mutual devotion fully and publicly satisfied. Dante and Beatrice. ("He had a wife, you know.") Shakespeare and the Dark lady of the sonnets. There were dozens of precedents, really, beautiful precedents that brought tears to the eye. Mr. Farley would literally kiss away her tears.

He never ceased being Mr. Farley to her. Oh, she would call him Harold because he insisted, but she never felt his equal. Pygmalion, that is what she was.

It was part of his plan that she should never worry after he was gone. He would provide for her, just as he would for his other daughters. She believed him. But she believed her instincts more. And her instincts told her she must have a baby if she was going to keep Mr. Farley.

He assumed, correctly, that she was on the pill, but he did not want to talk about it. It compounded his sin to use contraceptives. She did not tell him that she had decided to get pregnant. She wasn't sure if a man his age could have a child, though God knows he was vigorous enough in bed. When she was certain she was pregnant, she told him and his reaction was a shock.

"My God! What are you going to do?"

She assumed her Murillo Madonna expression.

"You mean to have it?"

"Don't you want me to?"

She could see that dark thoughts flew through his mind. His grip on her hand was painfully tight. But then he regained his composure.

"Of course you will have it." He took her in his arms and called her his darling girl, over and over, and everything was fine.

The story of John Dos Passos entered his repertoire now when he talked of precedents to their love. She would have her child; eventually all his children would know one another and be friends, just as Dos Passos came to know his legitimate older brother. Of course, her baby would be legitimate in a higher sense. God meant them to have a child. It was the only explanation. It was the only explanation that could reconcile him to her pregnancy.

She had her son. They had agreed to name a boy Sebastian, but the child died before there was time for a christening. He served the purpose anyway, making Harold Farley even more devoted to her.

Harold had not lived long enough to transmute their relation onto another plane. He did not live long enough to be reconciled with the Church. He died in her bed in Evanston. They had just finished making love; he lay back and sighed and that was it. It was a death like in the movies.

Her first reaction was horror. Her second, grief. Then came panic. But Harold had thought of everything. If ever anything went wrong, and she did not know what to do and he was not there to ask—but this had to be absolutely an emergency— she was to get in touch with his lawyer in Fox River, Amos Cadbury.

Mr. Cadbury seemed older than Harold, but June and the lawyer between them got the body dressed and down to her car and drove it to the municipal garage, where it took them twenty minutes to find his parked car. The keys to it were in the pocket of his coat. They transferred him to the backseat of the Continental, and Mr. Cadbury dismissed her wordlessly.

Harold Farley was found dead in his car in the parking lot behind his office. Sometime during the night, the car Mr. Cadbury had parked in front of her building disappeared. No question was raised about how Harold Farley had died, though someone must have wondered why his shorts were on backward. Getting them on at all had been a struggle and when they saw what they had done, Mr. Cadbury shook his head. They would have to stay like that.

June went to the funeral but kept out of the way. His widow was disconsolate, his daughters stunned and red-eyed. June felt a combination of them all. After the body was taken away to the cemetery, she stayed in the church, talking to God, asking Him to take care of Harold; he had been such a good man.

Death had come for Harold Farley before he made arrangements for June's future.

—— Eighteen ——

Cy was in Keegan's office when the last lab report came in. There was no sign that Connie Rush had been in her husband's office. The prints on the ashtray weren't hers and neither were those on the lipstick Agnes had found. Her prints weren't anywhere else in the office either.

"Almost too neat," Keegan said, but Cy could see the captain was relieved.

Wortman from the lab just stared at Keegan with lidless eyes. It was against Wortman's religion to make anything of the facts arrived at in the lab. Whatever Keegan wanted to think was okay with him.

"That all, Captain?"

"How fresh were the prints on the lipstick?"

"Old. Maybe months."

"Did the place look wiped?"

Wortman shook his head. "No."

"Was it?"

The corners of Wortman's mouth dimpled slightly. "No."

"That must be why. It was a good job."

But Wortman was impervious to sarcasm.

"Thanks, Jerry."

"Anytime."

Wortman opened the door without getting the tips of his fingers on any surface.

"What do you think, Cy?"

"That she didn't kill her husband."

"Drop the charges?"

Cy nodded. Keegan got out a cigar and settled back, and Cy knew he was meant to stay.

"Do you know, Cy, I was beginning to think she might have done it."

"So was I."

"Would we just drop charges if she wasn't someone we knew?"

"Yes."

"You're sure?"

Cy said he was sure. He did not smile. It was pretty obvious that Agnes had gotten to Keegan with her teasing.

"How long have you known the Farley family, Cy?"

"I always knew who they were in the parish. Nothing more than that. We were in a lower class than the Farleys."

"It was pretty hard not to know who they were, wasn't it? Him the chief usher every Sunday at the ten. You ever go to the ten?"

Cy had gone to six o'clock Mass after he finished delivering papers. That paper route had represented a significant fraction of the Horvath family income. His father was dead, his mother had a houseful of kids, Cy was the oldest. He had a paper route, he was a carry-out boy at the supermarket, he shoveled snow and raked leaves when he got the chance, making a crew of his younger brothers. Welfare? You didn't mention that word in the Horvath house. His mother knitted and crocheted things for babies, she babysat a lot. Cy vetoed her plan to hire herself out a few hours every day to clean other people's houses. Enough was enough. Every year the younger kids earned more money. Cy had been a great high school football player despite his schedule, but he turned down an athletic scholarship and went to work full time in the supermarket, waiting until he was old enough to take the police exam. He made certain each of his brothers and sisters finished high school at least. Three had graduated from college as well.

He said, "I usually went to the six."

"The six? Were you out jogging or what?"

"Something like that."

"If you'd gone to ten you'd have seen Mr. Farley walking the center aisle and his wife and daughters in the front pew."

Keegan seemed to be a big admirer of the late Mr. Farley, and he was obviously disappointed that Cy had not seen more of the man.

"He died funny, didn't he?"

"He was found dead in his car."

"I remember now. A heart attack?"

"Cy, while you're doing errands why don't you check out the coroner's report."

"Sure."

Well, everybody got a wild idea once in a while, and Keegan was entitled to his quota. Maybe it was part of the relief he felt that he didn't have to bring murder charges against a fellow parishioner and daughter of a man he admired. That was one thing about St. Hilary's that had stayed true even during the bad years before Roger Dowling was appointed pastor. For a time there had been a constant turnover of Order priests, Franciscans, a Marist, another Franciscan. None of them had acted as if it was a permanent job. Still, people had stuck together, the ones who didn't panic and sell and leave, that is. It was important to the parish that people like the Farleys stayed. Amos Cadbury had stayed, too.

An hour later, pursuing a wild idea of his own before he pursued Keegan's, Cy got out the report he had written of his interview with Edna Hospers. There was something about her description of the woman who had come for the Rush baby that morning that teased his mind. It was not a description of either Constance or Elizabeth Farley. Cy closed his eyes and waited for the description to fit someone else. He was certain it did, and someone he knew, someone he had met.

"Are you praying or asleep?" Agnes asked.

"Neither." He kept his eyes closed. "Give me the description of the woman who came for the Rush baby this morning."

"Didn't you hear we're dropping charges?"

"Yes."

"Pretty fast decision, wasn't it?"

"To arraign her? I suppose, but Keegan knows her and we have to be careful."

"That isn't what I meant."

"Did that description ring a bell with you, Agnes?"

"I was excluding, not including."

"I know. But who do you suppose it is?"

"I know who it sounds like."

"Who?"

"It doesn't make sense."

"Tell me."

"That big, big lady I had to pry you away from in the Fenwick Mall."

That was it! Dunn's receptionist. June. The description could have fit lots of people, of course, but it was Edna's mentioning that the woman turned sideways and looked at you like a bird when she spoke that did it.

"Maybe she's afraid of bad breath," Agnes said.

"Maybe."

"You don't think so."

"It's flirty. A come-on. Same with the way she puts her hand on your arm and leans close."

"On *your* arm, Lieutenant Horvath. You're the one who brings this out in her. Anyway, someone who looked like Betty Boop picked up the Rush baby this morning."

"Yeah. Her name is June."

"And I got the distinct impression from Captain Keegan that now that the infant is back where he belongs, we can stop worrying about it."

Liz Farley had said she would change her story and claim to have picked up the baby after all, so what could they do? Liz and her mother wanted no more fuss. Cy figured they had to be a hundred times more relieved than Keegan that the charges against Connie had been dropped.

"We still have a murder on our hands."

"So what do we do next?"

Get the coroner's report on old Mr. Farley? That would have to wait. That was as much a nostalgia trip for Keegan as a genuine inquiry.

"Let's go to the Fenwick Mall."

"You never get enough of that wonderful stuff, do you?"

"Check out the lipstick. We'll take it along."

There was a sale on in most stores at the mall, something called the mid-spring sale. ("Sounds like arrested motion," Agnes said.) Throngs of people with a consumerist gleam in their eye, the benches occupied mainly by old people, kids antsy as the end of school approached. Lots of people have said lots of things about malls, and most of them are true. They have taken the place of the town pump; they are what downtown was fifteen, twenty years ago. The Fenwick Mall was well designed, looking like the superstructure of an aircraft carrier with the huge parking lots its deck.

"I hate malls," Agnes said.

"You're supposed to."

"Come on."

"It brings you back. Besides, there's nowhere to go but to another mall."

"That's what I hate."

"I know."

"Oh, shut up. Are we going to arrest Betty Boop?"

"In mid-spring."

She hit his arm, hard.

"You go talk to the manager, I'll take the second-floor offices."

"Such self-sacrifice."

"Or the other way round, if you want."

"No, I'll take the manager. I like the slope of his forehead."

"He was a pretty good football player once."

"Then he wore a helmet."

Dunn's receptionist was seated at her desk, filing her nails, Walkman headphones over her thick hair.

"Is there a ball game on?" Cy asked.

"I'm listening to a tape."

But the whole building pulsed with muted music. Cy mentioned this.

"I know. It drives me crazy."

Cy picked up the featherweight headphones. "May I?"

"Be my guest."

Classical music. Well, well.

"Who is it, Fred Waring?"

She smiled tolerantly. "That is Antal Dorati conducting and the music is Beethoven."

141

"It is better than the other stuff."

"Anything is. But this is good. What brings you back?"

"We've dropped charges against Rush's wife."

"Oh."

"I thought I'd come tell you since you saw her here. There's no evidence she was in the office."

"Evidence?"

"Like fingerprints."

"You must have found mine in there. I've been inside. We're very neighborly here on Winners Row."

"If we found yours, we wouldn't know. They have to be on record."

She squinted at him. "Is that why you're here? To take my prints?"

"No. We're back to square one and I thought it might be useful to talk with you again."

"Where's your partner?"

"Talking with the manager."

"Then it isn't just me."

"How do you mean?"

"Well, it could be an excuse. 'I'd like to talk to you again, lady.'" She said this in a gruff voice.

"I'm a married man."

"Yes?"

"Don't you think that means anything?"

"I think it should. It doesn't always."

"Is this his day off?"

She leaned forward and Cy lifted his eyes. After all, he had brought up the fact that he was a married man.

"He doesn't take days off. You know someone who needs a dentist? Send them over."

"Does he have a patient with him now?"

"What he has is a miniature TV set he watches while supine in his dental chair."

"Supine?"

"Flat on his back."

"You're a surprising person, June, do you know that? That music, your vocabulary."

"You remember my name. And you like my mind. I know, you're a married man. So was Rush. Until the divorce, that is."

"Did he make a play for you?"

"Is water wet?"

Cy brought the little zip-lock plastic bag from his pocket and held it up. "That yours?"

"Where did you find it?"

"In Rush's office."

She looked at him. "Now I'm glad I already told you I've been there."

"You ever go out with him?"

"We had some meals together. He had no culture, no mind, no ideas. All he was was shrewd. And now he's dead."

"Classical music would have saved him?"

"Maybe not. Do I get my lipstick back?"

"Not right away."

"Is it evidence?"

"Of what?"

She turned her head sideways. "Where did you find it?"

"In his couch."

"Oh-oh."

"Where you seek financial advice is your own business. Now that his wife has been released, who do you think killed him?"

"They could form a line."

"His creditors? They're not likely to kill the goose until he lays the golden egg."

They had checked out Agnes's guess that Rush borrowed from the wrong people. Nothing.

"You'll have to ask his friends," June said.

"He didn't have any."

"Isn't that sad?"

"June what?"

"Slate."

A fruitless visit? Not at all. He had found out more than he had hoped. She had gone out with Rush, and more than once. Her reaction to hearing that her lipstick had been found in Rush's couch suggested that something more than passing the time of day had taken place. Cy had an idea that June Slate was going to be of more help in this case.

"Come on back," she said.

"I have to return your lipstick."

And he went downstairs to find Agnes Lamb.

—— Nineteen ——————

There were cousins in California, but the link was the thinnest one of blood. They had seen Peter Rush only once in their lives. They accepted the news but not the responsibility. Roger Dowling could hardly blame them.

"Would you say a Mass for his soul, Father?"

"Yes, of course."

"Where should I send the stipend?"

"That won't be necessary."

"Father, I'm a poor man, but I feel I ought to do something. My own cousin, after all."

145

The man sounded as if he had just de-planed from Aer Lingus. Or was he simply in the grips of what was now polysyllabically called ethnicity?

He took the matter to the Farleys. Liz tried to keep distaste from her expression, Connie's eyes widened and filled with agonized tears. "Oh my God, a funeral?"

"Since we cannot praise him," Mrs. Farley said. "We must bury him."

"Will it be public, Father?" Liz asked.

Mrs. Farley followed it up. "Could we avoid anything sensational? After what has happened, this is hard."

"For heaven's sake," Connie said. "He's dead."

"And you're sorry?"

"Sorry? The way my life is turning out? I wouldn't mind being dead myself."

"Constance!" Mrs. Farley said firmly. "If you can't control yourself, go to your room."

"My room? I feel I've flunked and have to repeat a year. Should I call myself Constance Farley again?"

"You would do well to remember you are a Farley. We will bury your husband with dignity and with as little fuss as possible. I assume it must be in the church.

146

We will put as good a face on it as we can. Whatever the silly courts say, you are his wife."

Mrs. Farley was somewhat more Catholic than the Church. Judge Jones could not put Constance Farley and Peter Rush asunder, but death both could and had. Nonetheless, Father Dowling was impressed by Mrs. Farley and by her daughters too. But the old woman particularly rose to the occasion, as if she had practiced the part. Whatever they knew or thought they knew of Peter Rush, his soul was now in the hands of God.

"We were married in that church," Connie said in an odd voice.

"So were your father and I." Mrs. Farley turned to Roger Dowling. "You will find that in the parish records, Father, if you still have them from all that time ago."

The records were in the rectory. It was surprising how much history had been put into half a dozen ledger-size books. When he first came to St. Hilary's, Father Dowling had gone through them, in the sense of turning over their leaves, as if the pages could acquaint him with his new parish. But all those baptisms and weddings and funerals represented the silent majority, not the living population of the parish, although many of the names were still on the roster. That night he had the volume containing the Farley marriage on his desk when Phil Keegan stopped by.

"I feel I should start paying room and board."

"You're always welcome, Phil."

"What are you looking up?"

"The Farley marriage. She told me today she had been married in this church, and I thought I'd get it out. Dorothy Tracy was her maiden name, born here in Fox River. She and her husband were the same age."

Phil got settled in a favorite chair and lit a cigar. Its aroma would bring Marie Murkin in for a pro forma complaint and then she would offer the captain a beer.

"Is that the only kind of record the parish keeps?"

"Why?"

"When Farley was named a Knight of St. Gregory, his pastor would have had a say in it, wouldn't he?"

"More likely than not he would have been asked to write a letter testifying to the good character of the nominee, saying that he was indeed an outstanding layman, that

148

sort of thing. But he would have been nominated higher up. Shall we see what there is?"

There was a pale carbon of a letter written by Charles O'Neil, O.F.M., saying that Farley was a member in good standing of the parish of St. Hilary's and had been for many years. An exemplary and generous layman, active in the religious and social affairs of the parish. Father O'Neil added his own humble recommendation to those of the more distinguished. Yours faithfully.

"Of course he wouldn't have known Farley," Phil said. "Not really. O'Neil was one of those who were here for a few months, then gone. As I remember, he came on Friday nights and left Monday after saying an early Mass."

"No Mass on the other days?"

"One friar or another would pop in and say it. We were like a missionary parish."

St. Hilary's had indeed slipped almost entirely from the notice of the Chicago chancery. When Roger Dowling had returned from a sanatorium in Wisconsin, he had not rejoined the archdiocesan marriage court, thank God. But where to put him? He could still see the monsignor's finger slide westward on a map of the largest diocese in the world. "Ah, what have we here? Fox River."

He might have said Ars. This was exile indeed. But his exile had swiftly become his home. Roger Dowling felt more blessed in adversity than he ever had when he shone among the comers of the archdiocese, brilliant, a good degree in canon law, ecclesiastical preferment in his future. Drink had drowned such hopes. What a relief it was to know that he was where he would always be, doing the work for which he had been ordained.

He said in defense of his Franciscan predecessor, "He could have relied on general reputation."

"Oh, sure."

"I thought I smelled that thing," Marie said, standing in the door. She shielded her eyes with one hand, pretending to have difficulty seeing into the smoke-filled study. "Are you in there, Father?"

"I think Phil might like a beer."

"Why are you looking at records?"

"I've been looking at the Farley wedding entry."

Phil said, "Marie, do you remember a friar named O'Neil?" The word *friar* never failed to elicit bad memories from the housekeeper. Those had been dark days, and she was no fan of Franciscans.

"That one! He ate twice as much on weekends as Father Dowling does in a week. And he looked it. If he fell down he would roll. And the way he drank bourbon I thought he might."

"Marie," Father Dowling said. "We're not Methodists, you know."

"You should talk. Coffee, coffee, coffee. It will eat your insides out."

"When it does, I'll switch to bourbon."

Cy said, "O'Neil wrote a letter on Farley's behalf when he received his great honor."

"So?"

"Saying what a fine upstanding Catholic man he was."

"The Farleys are the salt of the earth. Even he would have seen that. Do you want a beer?"

"As long as you're up."

"You!"

"Your interest in Farley seems more than routine, Phil," Roger Dowling said when the beer had been brought and Marie had gone up to her apartment and the TV.

"Does it?"

"Phil."

"Look, it's a bad thing to say but it has been plaguing my mind, so just let me say it to you in confidence. I don't believe Farley ever received communion."

"How could you possibly know a thing like that?"

"Because he was always an usher at the ten o'clock. He directed everyone else to the communion rail a pew at a time, very orderly, but he never went near it himself. My daughter noticed that first and I told her what you would tell me, but afterward I watched and it was true. Yet he was so visible in the church I doubt that anyone would have guessed it."

"An earlier Mass?"

"I don't say it's impossible."

"Well?"

"Wouldn't it be odd if a man who didn't really practice his religion were honored by the Church?"

"It would be unfortunate, I suppose. But he wasn't being canonized, Phil. There could be many explanations for what you noticed. Medical reasons. He might have been forbidden to fast."

"Even after the rules changed he stayed away. Surely he could have fasted for an hour."

Roger Dowling got them away from the topic. With great panache, Dante had assigned real people to hell and purgatory and paradise, but that was not an advisable practice for such nonpoets as himself and Phil Keegan. It is a sign of God's mercy that we do not know who did and who did not respond to His mercy. Except of course for the saints.

But Phil's speculation had a police motivation rather than a theological one. And it did cast new light on the Farley family, particularly on old Mrs. Farley. Tragedy lurks in the oddest places. Roger Dowling's own curiosity had been piqued.

"The funeral is tomorrow, Phil."

"Won't you be saying the noon Mass?"

"I have a substitute coming in." A Franciscan, but there was no need to mention that.

"Will the Farleys attend?"

"Of course."

"What time?"

"Nine o'clock."

Phil only nodded, but Roger Dowling would have bet that he would be there.

He had arranged for a private wake with McGinnis, just the Farley women there for the rosary. Closed coffin. Afterward, Mrs.

Farley asked McGinnis if she could view the body.

McGinnis was delighted in the ghoulish way of the undertaker. What an art it is whose artifacts are swiftly buried. Like carving in ice. Father Dowling stood beside Mrs. Farley when McGinnis lifted the top half of the cover. It was Roger Dowling's first view of Peter Rush. And the last. He had formed an idea of the man, not a very flattering one, but there was little of the gutsy egoist left in these mortal remains prettied up by McGinnis. The undertaker seemed to be waiting for comments. The best Dowling could manage was a nod.

"It doesn't look at all like him," Mrs. Farley said. McGinnis stirred uneasily, but she went on. "His mouth is closed."

So much for the private obsequies of Peter Rush. His widow had already left the room when Mrs. Farley asked to see the body. All in all, it was an ordeal for the Farley's, the only mourners for a man who had publicly humiliated them for months.

Father Dowling let the Farleys go ahead and asked McGinnis if there had been any visitors. McGinnis summoned a professional look of despair at the waywardness of men. None.

"Those flowers were sent, however."

Roger returned to the casket and to the rather elaborate wreath. A card. "Requiescat in pace. J." J? He noted that the florist was Shannon's, a large concern with branches throughout the Chicago area.

"We provided the rest," McGinnis added unctuously.

"Very nice."

The Farleys awaited him in the parking lot, and Mrs. Farley asked if he would care to come home with them for iced tea or whatever.

"Is coffee included in the whatever?"

"That won't be much of an Irish wake for Peter."

At the house, the two daughters eventually left Roger alone with Mrs. Farley.

"Father, I feel we're doing both too little and too much for him."

"You've done just the right thing."

"I can't help but remember my husband's funeral. What an occasion that was. One of the auxiliary bishops in the sanctuary. I don't know how many priests. Knights of Columbus and of St. Gregory in full regalia. It made you wonder if this is really a democracy."

"And I don't imagine it made it any easier to endure either."

"On the contrary. Our lives had become so public—at least his had—that any other kind of funeral would have put the whole burden on me. As it was, though much was made of the grieving widow, I felt almost superfluous. A successful husband is something of a stranger in his own home."

"I will say Mass for him this week."

"Thank you, Father. I pray for him every day. He died in his parked car, a heart attack, and wasn't found until hours had passed. He might have lived if he had been taken to the hospital immediately. God moves in mysterious ways."

"He is a merciful God."

"I count on that, Father. I do. Does it bore you to have people confide in you?"

"Not at all. But the best consolation is to be had in the confessional."

She looked at him, her mouth opening slightly, and burst into tears. For a minute she sobbed helplessly, then abruptly it was over.

"Father, sometimes I worry so about him."

"Pray for him and don't worry. God is merciful."

But she knew that He is also just. If Phil Keegan was correct in his suspicion about Mr. Farley's never receiving communion, the reason could well have been that he was not in the state of grace. Living in sin.

The phrase, perhaps not without reason, had come to have a single meaning.

—— Twenty ——

Edna Hospers did not want to do it. For one thing, she was too busy with her job at St. Hilary's, looking after the senior program and raising her kids. She never mentioned the fact that her husband was imprisoned at Joliet—maybe she still resented Lieutenant Horvath's part in putting Gene there. Of course she did.

"And anyway, what happens if she is the one? Do I point a finger and say she did it?"

"You don't do anything. You just go in and ask for an appointment."

"What if he's free?"

"Have your teeth cleaned. Have X rays taken. The department will pay for it."

"Socialized medicine, huh? Lieutenant, I just don't have the time."

"Look, I'm not going to arrest her."

"Then what's it all about?"

"I don't like loose ends. The baby's back, everybody's happy, but I want to know what went on and why. Maybe charges should be made if she's the one, but I don't make those decisions." He stopped to breathe. That was as long a speech as he made.

"Maybe the dentist is in on it. Did you see Laurence Olivier in *Marathon Man?*"

"You don't owe me any favors. Father Dowling thought you'd do it."

Her manner changed completely. "If Father Dowling wants me to do it, I'll do it."

"I'll go ask him."

"I thought you had!"

"An oversight."

To Horvath's surprise, Roger Dowling was not enthusiastic. He was in a hurry, he had a funeral in ten minutes, but he had his doubts.

"Cy, every time I ask Edna to do something above and beyond, something happens. I just can't ask her to do anything else."

"Captain Keegan thought you'd cooperate."

"Why didn't he call me?"

"He's going to."

Dowling shook his head and looked out over the playground for a minute. "Will you be with her?"

"Yes."

He turned and looked at Cy. "All right."

Back to the school Horvath went with the magic word.

"When will we go?" she asked, not happy about it.

"The sooner we go, the sooner you're back here."

"You don't even know if he is in today."

"I know he is in every day."

A tall old gent with his mouth open and an oversized Adam's apple seemed to be everywhere Cy turned. The guy looked familiar, too.

"Say, don't I know you?"

"What's your name?"

"Horvath. Fox River Police." And then he placed the guy. "And you're Tom Pouce. I thought you worked around the courthouse."

"Now and then."

"I hope you haven't retired, a man your age."

"Out making an arrest, Lieutenant?" He

moved from side to side as he said this, grinning.

"Yeah. You!" Cy whipped out the cuffs and the old guy yelped and jumped back.

"What for? What have I done?"

Cy began to wonder. He put away the cuffs. "Never kid a kidder."

Old Tom shambled away in an odd skipping walk, his head turned, keeping an eye on Horvath. Edna Hospers came out of her office.

"How long has old Tom Pouce been coming here?"

"Oh, I don't know exactly. More of late than before. He keeps to himself, sort of hovers around. That's all some of them want, company. But at a distance. They've stopped making new friends."

"I suppose."

"That's the kind that doesn't last."

For the first half of the drive to the mall, Edna was silent. No problem there: Cy wasn't much of a talker either. But then his silence seemed to get to her.

"Where's your partner?"

"Her day off."

"When's yours?"

"Today."

He knew that she had turned to stare

at him. "You really can't wait to find out if this is the woman, can you?"

"One way or the other, I'll have the rest of the day."

"Devoted public servant."

"No, you were right the first time. I want to know if my hunch is right."

"You going in with me?"

"Upstairs, but not into the office. I'll be in the hall."

"Why can't I just look in? That's all it would take. I'll know if she's the one."

"You don't want her to see you."

"Not particularly. The baby's safe, isn't he? What did she do that I didn't do?"

"She's in no more danger than you are. Look, I don't care how you do it, just make it definite. But she's as likely to notice you looking in as going in."

"Still, it's different."

The thing that bothered Cy was the time. He had not counted on getting Edna Hospers's cooperation so quickly and it was only 9:45 as they approached the mall, even though he had driven like a snail. Well, if they had to wait, they would wait. Edna wouldn't back out now.

"There she is!" Edna cried as he pulled into an empty space near the entrance to the offices. Horvath looked where she was pointing and, sure enough, there was June Slate moving regally among the cars.

"You're sure?"

"Absolutely."

"Good enough." He put the car in reverse and started to back out.

"Is that all?"

"That's all."

"I guess I half wanted a little drama to go with it. Who is she?"

"A dentist's receptionist."

Edna made a face. "I already knew that."

"The dentist's office is across the hall from Peter Rush's."

"Aha," she said and, after a moment, "What does it mean?"

"I don't know."

"But you're not going to just forget her, are you? You never forget."

He said nothing. It wasn't meant as a compliment. He guessed she was thinking again of her husband in Joliet.

He had lied about taking the rest of the day off. He was getting as bad as Keegan, all work and no play. But then he was Keegan's protégé, handpicked to be his right-hand man. Edna Hospers was loyal to Father Dowling, and with good reason. Cy

Horvath had cause to feel the same toward Captain Keegan. After he dropped Edna off, he headed for the coroner and a belated look at the autopsy report on Mr. Farley. Once that was done, he could assuage his own curiosity.

Sweeney the coroner always wore a smile, but it was expressive of dyspepsia rather than good humor. Dyspepsia! It was a wonder he could eat at all.

"I never eat on the job." A joke.

Cy had watched Sweeney at work, describing in great detail and with some relish whatever he was doing, speaking into the microphone hanging over the table on which he worked. The whir of saw and whine of drill could test the strongest stomach. The first time he had acted as Sweeney's acolyte (the coroner's term), he got through it by promising himself he would never do it again. Even if it meant returning to a beat, he would never do this again.

"Farley, Harold. Sure. Why not?" He picked up his phone, pressed a button and said, "Thelma, bring me the file on my desk. Farley, Harold."

After he put down the phone, he placed both hands on his stomach and looked at Horvath with narrowed eyes.

"You've lost weight."

"I've been running."

"Don't," Sweeney said. "I had nine joggers last year, brought in still wearing their track suits. Thought they were going to live forever, be sound as a dollar. Nonsense. It's all in your genes. Unless you get run over or murdered. Maybe those are in the genes, too."

"My wife won't let me wear jeans when I run."

"Ho ho."

Thelma brought in the file and Sweeney flipped it open. "What are you looking for?" He began to read from the report, a transcript of what he had dictated while performing the autopsy. Cy held up his hand.

"Not that kind of thing."

"That's the kind of thing we deal with here."

"He died of what?"

"An aneurysm. Know what that is?"

"Vaguely. Anything funny about his death?"

"Yes."

"What?"

"Two things. First, he had his shorts on backwards."

Cy laughed. "You're kidding."

"I never kid."

"Backwards? How could that happen?"

"Maybe he turned around too fast. I lied about not kidding. They were boxer shorts, too. No way he could do peepee wearing those wrong side front. A mystery. But we encounter many mysteries here."

"You said there were two things."

"Yes. Maybe it was the shorts that suggested it, but I concluded he had not died in the position he was found in. They found him seated behind the wheel of his car."

"Didn't you mention these things at the time?"

Sweeney waved the folder. "It's all here."

"Can I have a copy of that?"

"I can't tell them what to do, Lieutenant. I can only tell them what I find."

"Do you think there was foul play?"

"No more than with Nelson Rockefeller." Sweeney explained what he meant.

"Any recent sexual activity?"

Sweeney opened the folder again. "There was semen in the urethra."

Cy waited for Thelma to make a copy of Sweeney's report. He did not know what to make of this. There should have been an investigation at the time Sweeney submitted his report. Thank God Agnes wasn't here.

He checked up on June Slate the hard way, going slowly back through city directories. She had had the same address since 1984. Before that, she wasn't in the book. He kept at it and eventually she showed up again, in the early 70s, an apartment building close to downtown. Just the one year. He checked the book for the previous year but she was not listed. For nearly ten years she had disappeared from the Fox River phone book. Cy put through a call to Chicago, asked for records, and gave the name. The clack of a computer keyboard came over the line.

"Would you identify yourself, sir?"

He gave her the code that told her he was a police detective.

"We have a listing in that name in Evanston from 1974 until 1984."

"Let me have the address, will you?"

He wrote it down, telling himself it meant nothing. So she had lived in Evanston during those years. There must be some inexpensive housing in Evanston.

—— Twenty-One ——

Phil Keegan had been to some pretty miserable funerals in his time, but Peter Rush's hit a new low.

There were always a few extras around for weddings and funerals, usually old women who seemed to spend half the morning in church and, since they were there anyway, why not sit in on a nice wedding or funeral? This morning the extras outnumbered the principal mourners by three to one. And that ratio was achieved only because Keegan included himself among the mourners. So far as he knew, he had never seen the man alive.

The Farley women were there, of course, and McGinnis and one of his helpers, looking sad, wringing their hands, the usual thing. McGinnis's hair looked more like cotton from a bottle than it usually did. The man could have been a ballroom dancer, a saxophone player, a waiter, if it hadn't been for that phony expression. He tried to shoo some old women up into front pews, but they were having none of that. Once things got under way, McGinnis would slip outside for a cigarette.

Roger Dowling was his usual dignified self at the altar and his homily, while generic, was apt. He would not say anything directly of the deceased, since he had never known him personally, but death by violence must bring home to each of us the precariousness of human life. We are ever in the hands of God, whether we acknowledge it or not. We can do nothing without Him. Most fundamental of all, we would not exist if He did not sustain us at every moment. Flimsy as he is, however, man has an eternal destiny. Peter was so called, as are we all. So let us think of that this morning as we offer prayers for the repose of his soul. Doubtless he was a sinner, like you and me. Like us, he stood in need of the grace of God. Let us pray now that God will have mercy on his soul.

It was okay, Phil thought, at the moment not feeling particularly mortal. As much as anything else, his wife's death had surprised him. It still surprised him when he thought about it. He listened to Roger and supposed the homily applied to him, but he did not feel it.

It got to Mrs. Farley, though. She dabbed at her eyes and her shoulders lifted and fell. Her two daughters looked straight ahead. They were performing a duty and the sooner it was done the better.

Keegan went along to the cemetery, the cortege thus including three cars. The drive induced thought. Peter Rush had been trying to get money out of the Farleys. Well, he got the price of a funeral, anyway. After the graveside ceremony, Phil asked Roger if he would like a ride back to the rectory.

"I hoped you'd ask. McGinnis is not a stimulating companion. He would want to discuss my homily or, worse, compliment me on it."

"It wasn't bad."

"Thanks for the fulsome praise."

"You want to ride with McGinnis, go ahead."

"Actually I want to talk to you, Phil."

Keegan called in on the drive to St. Hilary's and was told that Horvath wanted to see him.

"Horvath? It's his day off. Put him on."

Cy's voice crackled through. "You coming back to your office?"

"Aren't you off today?"

"I followed up on a couple things."

"Come on out to St. Hilary's. I'll wangle you an invitation to lunch." He looked at Roger, who nodded.

"Roger," Cy said.

"That's right." But his passenger didn't see the joke. "Over and out."

Roger said, "Cy was at the parish before the funeral Mass. He wanted Edna Hospers to identify the woman who picked up little Timothy Rush the second time."

"He must be on to something."

"I was reluctant to get Edna Hospers any more involved than she already is."

"Maybe it didn't work out. The identification."

"Would he want to see you if it hadn't?"

One of Horvath's great merits was doggedness. He wouldn't quit till he identified the mysterious woman who picked up the baby and threw everyone into momentary panic. She had been reenacting the original phony kidnapping. Why?

"That does make it interesting," Roger agreed. "Connie said she staged the kidnapping to make a point to her husband. What was the point the second time? It would seem to be directed at Connie, wouldn't it?"

When Horvath arrived, few would have guessed he was excited about anything. But he did not start right in on the mystery woman.

"You wanted me to check on Farley's autopsy."

They were in the study while Marie faced the welcome challenge of two unexpected guests.

"What did you find, Cy?"

"I got a copy of Sweeney's report. He doesn't think Farley died in his car or in a seated position anywhere. He thinks the body was moved."

"Why the hell didn't he say so at the time?"

"He says he did."

"Well, this is the first I've heard of it."

"What would you have done?" Roger asked.

"I don't know," Phil said. "Not nothing, I can tell you that. Who did he send the report to?"

"*We* have no copy," Cy said. "I checked."

"Robertson! Does Agnes Lamb know about this?"

"No."

"She will. And I will agree with what she says then. Chief Robertson should have told us this. I assumed the autopsy showed the obvious. The man got into his parked car, then had a fatal heart attack. He wasn't discovered for hours. Learn a lesson, Cy.

171

Never assume anything where Robertson is involved. Anything else?"

"There were signs of recent sexual activity. Sweeney thinks he may have died in bed. A funny thing. His shorts were on backwards."

"What!"

Cy repeated it, deadpan. Phil looked at Roger Dowling and they started laughing at the same time. Even Cy smiled. Of course it was not funny at all.

"Sweeney guesses someone dressed him after he died?"

"Sweeney never guesses."

"His whole job is guessing."

"He says he deals in facts."

"Thank God he does," Roger Dowling said.

Marie called them to table and during lunch Cy let the rest of it out. The woman who picked up the Rush baby was June Slate, receptionist for a dentist named Dunn, who practiced in the Fenwick Mall across the hall from Peter Rush's office. Before going to work for Dunn, the receptionist lived in a luxury apartment in Evanston. Cy handed Keegan a card. "The rental agent."

"Amos Cadbury!"

"Our Amos Cadbury?" Roger asked.

"Did you talk to him?" Keegan asked.

"Not yet."

"Good. We don't want to be rash." Cy looked at him, and although his expression did not change, he might have been Agnes Lamb. "Before we do, I want to know her job record. How long she been working for Dunn?"

"I don't know."

"I'd like to see the application she made out for that job."

"We could ask Dunn."

"Cy, do you get the impression that she's the key? An awful lot of things link up to her. Peter Rush. The Rush baby. Now Cadbury. I want to know a lot about her before we talk with Cadbury. He could just tell us he hasn't any idea who the tenants are in property he controls in Evanston, and we would have to do then what we should do first."

From St. Hilary's he and Cy went to the apartment house June Slate had lived in in the early 70s in Fox River. It was called the Crestview, though any crest it had a view of had disappeared when the highways were cut through. The place was like a sorority house or YWCA, a haven for single working girls. And the short squinty woman with dyed blond hair, who looked at them first through her upper lenses, then the lower, Mrs. Chase, had worked right here since she herself was a girl.

"You keep records?"

"With my memory, I don't need them, but yes, I keep records." She worked her mouth a bit and smiled. "What sort of police work do you do?"

"All kinds. Do you remember June Slate?"

She tipped back her head, closed her eyes and began to move her lips. "That's at least ten years ago."

"1973," Cy said helpfully.

Her eyes opened and she smiled. "Yes, I remember her. A nice girl. Came from California, as I remember. You'd think the traffic went the other way, wouldn't you?"

"Where did she work?"

"Now that I would have to look up."

And she did. She reminded Keegan of Father Dowling poring over the parish records. And then she had it.

"She worked for Farley Enterprises right downtown. She didn't stay very long."

"At Farley's?"

"I meant here."

They thanked Mrs. Chase and went out to the car without speaking. Cy drove them back to the rectory, where Keegan had left his car. Briefly Roger extracted the captain's promise that he would be kept informed, then concentrated on June Slate and her link to Mr. Farley himself.

The question was: What the hell did it mean?

—— Twenty-Two ——

The sight of Pete's closed and locked office door oppressed her. She even wished the police were still poking around. At least they had provided some excitement. This morning Dunn had three appointments, something in itself, but that kept him busy, not her. Later, in the afternoon, there were some kids coming. The kids were what made the job difficult. They reminded her of her own child. They had decided to call him Sebastian if it was a boy and Laura if it was a girl. What fun it had been making plans. He said it made him feel young again. They had planned everything. Or so it had seemed. What they had not planned on was spina bifida. But that was what the baby had.

She knew exactly how old he would be now, if he had lived. They had wanted a baby so much, but they did not want a baby with spina bifida. The whole thing seemed to take place in code. Nobody came right out and said it. Her baby was and then her baby was no more. Very clinical. Very discreet. And very, very depressing.

After all that waiting, to return to the apartment with nothing. She had never felt lonely there before, but now it seemed just a lot of rooms, too many for one person. And Harold the Catholic took it far worse.

He wouldn't talk about it at first. It was as though nothing had happened. It got to her, as if he was by his silence trying to get her to think it had all been a dream: her pregnancy, the happy months of planning, going to the hospital and then the grim news. Harold had told her. Harold had made the decision and he would never forgive himself for it.

For the first time since she had known him, he drank too much; only once, but it was enough. The malformed baby was a punishment. This had come forth from deep within him, needing the brandy to find its way out, and there it was. She would never have known if he had not gotten drunk. What a terrible thought, that God was keeping an eye on them and didn't like what they were doing, Harold being married and all, so He punished them with a defective child. Why? So Harold would stop seeing her?

If that had been the divine plan, it did not work. They were closer after the loss of the baby than they had been before. Partners in crime? She didn't care. She needed him much more after returning empty-handed from the hospital, and he was even more gentle now. It went without saying that she would never get pregnant again. She could not have gone through that again for anything. From now on, her life would center on Harold alone.

But within a year he was dead and there was the awful business of getting him dressed and helping Mr. Cadbury carry him down to the car. And then to find later that he had not left her anything.

She had telephoned Mr. Cadbury, he had been Harold's lawyer, and asked about it. Cadbury was very formal, very polite.

"He spoke of that several times, yes. I know he intended to make the necessary changes. But he never got around to actually doing so."

"But he told you what he meant to do?"

"Yes, he did."

"Isn't that enough?"

"Oh my, no. Not at all. It would have had to be drawn up quite specifically and then signed. Above all, signed. That he never did."

"What am I to do?"

"I cannot advise you there."

He said she could stay on in the apartment in Evanston for another year. Then what? She would be on her own. She decided to be on her own immediately.

It was Pete who put her onto the job in Dunn's office. The previous girl was leaving to get married.

"It's right across from me. Great location."

"You mean the mall?"

"That too."

He was vulgar and a phony, just about everything Harold had not been. She first heard of him when he sued his wife for divorce, it was all over the papers and of course the Farley connection hit her. She went down to the courthouse to look on. After the session, when she saw Pete go across the street to a bar, she decided to have a drink herself. That is how they had met.

A pickup, he had called her, when he wanted to be mean, which was when he was drunk, which was often. Harold had never spoken an unkind word to her. Maybe that is the difference between older men and those closer to her own age. Pete was such a crazy mixture of tenderness and cruelty that he kept her off balance. It was one of his charms. But what she most liked was to get him going on the family into which he had married.

"What are the parents like?"

"Her father's dead." It seemed significant that even Pete spoke respectfully of Harold. But that had been a lapse, after all. "Starchy sonofabitch. And close with a buck? You'd think someone that rich would want to help his daughter's husband, wouldn't you? Forget it. I'll tell you one thing, though. If he were still alive they would be settling out of court. He would never have let things go so far."

Of course, Pete preferred talking of his wife and what a nag she was. June didn't really blame her. It seemed never to strike Pete that he ought to take care of himself.

But he had married money and figured his troubles were over.

June resolved from the beginning that she would never tell Pete or anyone else of her connection to the Farley family.

Dear God, if only she had stuck to that resolution.

—— Twenty-Three ——

Marie came over to the church, where Father Dowling was saying his rosary before the Blessed Sacrament, to tell him Mr. Amos Cadbury had come to the rectory to see him. The priest nodded. He would finish the decade he was saying. The fifth joyful mystery. The finding of the child Jesus in the temple. Who had predicted that Connie Rush would be overjoyed at the return of her child?

Marie had shown Cadbury into the study, and the lawyer stood at a bookshelf, his glasses lifted to his forehead, peering at titles.

"A very interesting collection, Father," he said, putting out his hand.

"Completely random. Sit down, Mr. Cadbury. I have bought books over the

years since my seminary days, largely without plan."

"Isn't that the best kind of library?
Planned collections are seldom read."

"You may be right."

"I don't see a great deal on canon law."

"No. No. I didn't keep much in that line
when I moved here."

"Isn't your degree in canon law?"

"It is. I would have preferred going on
in theology, or even philosophy. But the
Cardinal wanted me to study canon law."

"So of course you did."

"Of course."

"One doesn't always find such docility
in priests nowadays."

"It was partly fear in my case. As for
rebels, it is the middle-aged ones who do
the damage. They haven't the excuse of
youth."

"I had hoped we could speak lawyer to
lawyer, as it were."

"Lawyer to priest is even better."

"I haven't come to make a confession
in the sacramental sense," Cadbury said
carefully. His silver hair was laid back
close on his narrow high-domed head.
Roger Dowling imagined the lawyer using
a pair of silver-backed brushes on it. "I

do have something I wish to tell you in confidence."

"Of course."

"Father, I have represented the Farley family for many years. Harold and I were boyhood friends. I knew his wife before they married. The four of us, Mrs. Cadbury included, knew one another all our lives."

"How long has Mrs. Cadbury been dead?"

"Three years. Her death was overshadowed by Harold's. But then the three of us could never compete with him."

"Now there is just Mrs. Farley and yourself."

"Yes."

"I thought your interest in the Farleys was more than professional."

"There are those who say Farley was blessed not to have lived to see what has happened recently."

"And what do you say?"

A cold expression appeared fleetingly on Cadbury's face. "It would not have happened if he had been alive."

"He died a strange death."

"He lived a strange life."

Roger Dowling sensed they had come to the point of Cadbury's visit. He waited.

The lawyer crossed his legs, adjusted the crease of his trousers, then looked directly at the priest.

"I tried to tell myself that he was schizophrenic, but I don't really believe in psychiatry. I have seen what it has done to courtroom procedures. I am an old-fashioned man, Father Dowling. I think we are responsible for what we do. Extenuating circumstances, yes. Some things merely happen, of course. But basically we must answer for what we do. . . . Farley led a double life. He kept a mistress for years in Evanston. I could not believe he would do this to his wife; the fact that she did not know does not signify. We talked about it thoroughly only once. He had an incredible rationale for his life. Allusions to Lope de Vega were prominent. I was looking for him on your shelves. At the time I did not know who Lope de Vega was."

"But you looked him up?"

"Against my will, he has become one of my own favorite authors. Farley's appeal to him could not stop that."

"You read him in Spanish?"

"I do."

"He became a priest late in life, did he not?"

"After fathering any number of bastard children. He had two wives besides. The poems he wrote after his conversion are among the most beautiful I know."

"Isn't that the libertine's hope—to live as he likes and, in the end, turn to God and make a holy death?"

"Farley was not so fortunate. He died in his mistress's bed in Evanston. She telephoned me, of course. Farley had always managed to compel me to aid him. After all, I was his lawyer. There are parallels in the life of Lope de Vega. I am not exculpating myself. I could have said no. I could have threatened to expose him. I did not. I went along. And I was loyal, if that is the word, even after his death."

"I can attest to that."

"I refer to something quite specific. When the woman in Evanston telephoned me in the middle of the night to tell me, with you can imagine what emotion, that Farley was dead in her bed, she said he had told her she could always expect help from me. I would help her. And I did."

Cadbury moistened his lips. His narrative voice was one he might have used to describe his last game of golf.

"I drove there and found that he was

indeed dead. Standing beside that bed—O what a bower it was, all silk and soft hues, the lighting artful—and looking down at the dead body of my friend, I felt conflicting emotions. Sorrow, yes. But remorse, too, that I had not been a friend indeed and attempted to talk sense to him. But my fundamental feeling was anger. Even rage." Cadbury stroked his upper lip as if he expected to find a mustache there. "He had made a mockery of his family and his religion. He accepted—sought—appointment as a Knight of St. Gregory, while keeping a mistress in Evanston. I felt anger at the way he had used me. The idea of letting him lie there was tempting. I could call the police and say that a man had died in the apartment of one of my tenants. You see, I own the building. When I rented the apartment to Farley I had no idea he would use it as he did. He gave me to understand that one of his daughters was thinking of attending Northwestern. So I thought of letting him be seen for what he was, if only posthumously. Of course I could not. Almost before I knew what I was doing, I said a prayer for him. Aloud. The woman, distraught, begging me to do something, must have thought I was crazy. It was the 'thought of something after death' that prompted me. I prayed that a last lucid moment had been granted him, during which he appealed for God's mercy and received it."

"I hope that is what happened."

"But we both know how unlikely death-bed conversions are. And when the death-bed is the couch of a mistress, well . . ."

"What did you do?"

"We dressed him, the girl and I. That is far more difficult than it sounds. A dead body is a dead weight. I suppose that is the origin of the phrase. We managed, despite her hysteria, to get it done. Then I carried the body of my friend down a flight of stairs to the garage. Farley's car was parked in a municipal garage. That was his first cortege, the girl and I in her car carrying Farley's body to his. I wanted him found as far from Evanston as possible, in Fox River. I got him behind the wheel of his car. I shall never forget my last look at my friend. He sat rigid and wide-eyed behind the wheel, staring into eternity.

"That was a risky thing to do."

"Legally, yes. But I had done far worse things for him in the name of friendship, so why balk at that? I had colluded with him in the deception of his wife and she, too, was a dear friend."

"Did she ever suspect her husband's double life?"

"I cannot believe she didn't. She is an intelligent woman. To this day she has an acute mind. It is inconceivable to me that a spouse would not suspect a long-term affair."

"Did she ever say anything?"

The question horrified Cadbury. "She would have been even less likely to mention it, if she knew, than I was. You have to understand, Father, that being Catholic was bred into us from the cradle, into my wife and his, into Farley and myself. We were in the world but not of it. Marriages might degenerate all around us into episodes of convenience, unrelated to having a family, dissoluble at will, but we had married in the Church. The ceremony put into elevated terms the meaning of our love. For better, for worse, for richer, for poorer, in sickness and in health, till death do us part. That was as elementary as the alphabet. Even if, which God forbid, one's spouse went mad or to love or whatever, the bond remained. I regard that belief as the cement of society. Permanence of marriage, children, a life lived under the eye of God." Cadbury spoke with muted, self-deprecating eloquence. Then his tone changed. "That is what Farley mocked with his deeds. That he had done what he had was bad enough; for it to be known and to give scandal would be worse. I take full responsibility for moving his body."

"You have indeed proved a loyal friend."

"I fear I will pay for such loyalty. Inquiries have been made about that apartment in Evanston. Menacing inquiries."

"Does the woman still live there?"

"She refused my offer to stay on for a year after his death. Thank God she refused."

"Where is she now?"

"In Fox River. I have kept myself informed about her. She had reason to expect that Farley would leave her money. He intended to. But he never made the necessary changes in his will. That seemed a blessing, but I have always feared she would do something through the courts to make a claim on the estate. Recent rulings have set precedents. An effective case could be made for her. I would counsel settling out of court if such a claim were made. But by then the damage would be done, Mrs.

Farley would know. I have lived in fear of that woman talking to a lawyer who would be all too eager to file a suit."

"Why hasn't she?"

Cadbury blinked twice. "It could well be that, having loved him in life, having benefited from their relationship then, she does not want to injure him in death."

"An interesting woman."

"She is. She is also what her long liaison with Farley would suggest. Unconventional, let us say. My fears returned, more strongly, when she began to see Peter Rush."

"Connie's husband?"

Cadbury nodded. "This was quite recent. During the infamous trial. Every imaginable legal antic was pressed into service by that unconscionable man and his lawyers. Imagine asking the wife he wanted to divorce to support him! In such company, the girl would be bound to think of legal recourses open to her."

"What is her name?"

Cadbury stiffened in surprise. Then a small smile came and went. "Why should I cavil at that? June Slate."

Father Dowling sat back in his chair. "Who works for a dentist named Dunn in the Fenwick Mall?"

"How odd that you should know that."

"Mr. Cadbury, she is the woman who picked up little Timothy the other morning and then left him in church a second time."

"How do you know this?"

"The police know."

Cadbury's olive complexion went gray. "I see."

"They know of her friendship with Peter Rush. They know about the apartment in Evanston. They know you own it."

"Dear God."

"There is more. They suspect Farley's body was moved after he died and that he had recently been with a woman."

"How can they know that?"

"You put his shorts on backwards."

Cadbury looked at the priest. "It is a wonder we got them on at all. Well. Then the police will soon be piecing together this whole wearisome story. How ironic. I came to tell you all these dark secrets in order to enlist your help."

"In what way?"

"June Slate should get something from the Farley estate. Elizabeth Farley realizes that."

"Then she knows?"

"Liz is no fool. She went over everything

after her father's death. He had tried to conceal the money going to Evanston under the guise of a small foundation. An educational foundation. Grants to help the needy pursue a higher education. The trail led her to the apartment. That in turn led her to me. We had a much abbreviated form of this conversation at that time."

"And she is amenable to a settlement being made?" It was hard not to adopt Cadbury's elegant mode of speech.

"She is. But now June Slate demurs. I have tried persuasion unsuccessfully. My thought was, perhaps if you spoke to her . . ."

"I would be glad to."

Cadbury acknowledged this by closing his eyes briefly. "It seemed far more of a solution before you told me what the police know."

"When may I talk with her?"

"She will not come to my office."

"Would she come here?"

"You must invite her yourself, Father. I am not an effective intermediary with her. If you gain her assent in principle, the details can be worked out. You may assure her it will be a large amount, enough to keep her for life."

"Do you have her telephone number?"

Cadbury took a slim leather notebook from an inner pocket of his suit jacket, allowed it to open as if it were a bird spreading it wings in his hand, took a slip of paper from it and placed it on the desk.

"You can see I came here with hope."

Roger Dowling took the paper and pulled the phone toward him. "I'll call her now."

"Use the second number, then. She will be at work."

—— Twenty-Four ——

Old Tom never thought Tuttle would give him the shaft, but that's what happened all right.

Big buddies so long as Tom had information, but now Tuttle was working on his own and to hell with Old Tom.

A lifetime of practice in accepting such treatment enabled Tom to chalk it up and go back to St. Hilary's school to kibitz on the old codgers playing 500. Cards. Stupid game. Little kids playing Old Maid, grownups playing bridge, please tell me where the difference lies. And shuffleboard. Games. It was the whole idea of games that bothered him. He felt a sharp pang of regret. How nice it would be to settle down in Tuttle's office with pop and pizza and talk over that one. Games, not sports. Sports were another thing. But games were simply a means of wasting time. Tom bet Tuttle would have a thing or two to say on the subject.

That lost chance for meaningful dialogue sent him wandering through the school, shuffling along the lower corridor, then up the stairs to the top floor and past the unused classrooms. Think of all the kids who had gone to school here. Then down the far steps, which brought him to the main corridor and on past Mrs. Hospers's office.

Did she suspect he was the one who had told on her? Why would she? As far as he knew, nothing had happened. In fact, the more Tom thought of what he had witnessed the other day, and duly reported to his supposed friend Tuttle, the more he wondered why nothing had happened. An abandoned baby and no consequences? Damn, but he wished Tuttle would answer his phone. The one time he had gotten through to him at his office, Tuttle had said, "Not now, Tom. Call me back." When he called back the phone was not answered. That was how it had been all day.

"Aren't you Tom Pouce?"

He jumped. Mrs. Hospers had come out of her office, and there they were face to face.

"That's my name."

"What's your game?"

"Huh?"

"What did you do?"

"Did? I worked for the railroad, that's what I did. What I *do* is something else."

She smiled. She was just the kind of woman you would trust with an abandoned baby.

"I work down at the courthouse off and on, doing things for lawyers."

"So that's why you're not here as much as others."

"You run a good program."

"Why, thank you."

"Can I make a suggestion?"

"Of course."

"I'd introduce some talking sessions. Seminars. Men sitting around with a definite topic to talk about it."

"Only men?"

"Have one for women, too, though they don't need the encouragement as much."

"I'll tell you what, Tom. I'll put you in charge. You work it out and come to me and we'll announce it. Seminars. Seminars for men, that is."

Off she went down the corridor and, watching her go, Tom felt wonderful. Why hadn't he thought of this before? He didn't need Tuttle. This place must be full of men with real experience of life. You put three, four, six of them around a table, and things could happen.

He took a tour of the former gym, where all the games were in progress, looking for possible participants in talk sessions. Better not suggest the topic of games right away. Tom was sure the idea would work. In fact, he felt so good he decided to try getting through to Tuttle again.

"Tuttle & Tuttle."

"This is Tom."

"I thought you were going to call me back."

"I did."

"I've been in and out."

"That's what I figured."

"When can we get together?"

"I don't know. I've been put in charge of something here."

"At St. Hilary's? Come on, Tom. Hang

around with those old coots and you'll become one yourself before you know it."

"When did you have in mind?"

"What's wrong with now?"

"Now is fine."

"Tom, you got any money, pick up some chow mein."

"I paid for the pizza," Tom said.

"I remember. I'll pay you when you get here."

Now there would be a bonus, actually getting some money out of Tuttle. Tom went looking for Mrs. Hospers to tell her he had been called downtown but would try to be back that afternoon. He found her behind the school, helping to put up the badminton net. She seem puzzled that he was telling her this.

"I won't forget the seminars," he promised.

"Oh good. I'm counting on you."

All the way downtown on the bus, riding free as a senior citizen, he felt good. Happy. Now there was a topic, happiness. One you could get your teeth into. Who doesn't have ideas about what it is that makes a person happy?

Tuttle was excited to see Tom, even more excited to see the chow mein.

"It cost two dollars and eleven cents."

"What a bargain! People on welfare eat Chinese food, they would probably gain weight. The reason I called you, Tom."

Tuttle interrupted himself with a plastic forkful of chow mein.

"I called you," Tom said.

Tuttle waved his hand as if to discourage irrelevancies. He swallowed. "Tom, I wanted you to be the first to know because you put me on to it, sort of."

Tom accepted this recognition and helped himself to chow mein. Tuttle already had sixty percent of it on his paper plate. Tom ate the rest out of the carton. Let Tuttle have all the noodles.

"I am about to take on a client who has a claim worth . . ." Tuttle paused as his darting eyes sought an adequate sum. "Hundreds of thousands of dollars."

"Who is it?"

Tuttle smiled. "Let us just say that she figured in the musical babies game out at St. Hilary's."

"She isn't your client yet?"

"She gonna turn down a chance for big money? Real big money?" Tuttle frowned at the thought. "What I don't understand is why no lawyer recommended this before."

"She's going to sue somebody."

"That's right."

"Who?"

Tuttle looked slyly at Tom, while licking his fork. "The Farley estate."

—— Twenty-Five ——————

Suddenly she was the most popular girl on the block. Two urgent calls from people who wanted to see her as soon as possible. Well, only the lawyer had called it urgent. The priest, Father Dowling, said he had something of importance to discuss with her.

"My soul?"

He laughed. A nice laugh. "That is always my ultimate interest, of course. But I had something less important in mind."

She couldn't say "My body?" Not to a priest. She had to stop talking like that. It had nothing to do with who she really was. It was a carryover from Pete.

"Since you sent flowers to the funeral home, I thought that might give us a starting point."

"How did you know that?"

"I guessed. You weren't at the funeral."

"No."

"But you know where St. Hilary's is, I hope. Can we get together?"

She told him she would come on her lunch hour. "I can be late getting back to work."

"What I have to say may make you decide not to go back."

"What does that mean?"

"Twelve-thirty?"

She agreed. He had made her curious, and then a little nervous. The lawyer had appealed only to her avarice and was easy to turn down.

"Don't you understand what I'm saying?" Tuttle had persisted. "We are talking hundreds of thousands of dollars."

"Not we. You."

"You hate money?"

"No, just lawyers."

"Are you represented?"

"In Congress?"

A pause before he gave it a token laugh. "I'm serious. Do you have a lawyer?"

"Yes."

"May I ask who it is?"

"Sure."

"Who is it?"

"I won't tell you."

She had him placed now. Tuttle. The little guy in the Irish tweed hat who had offered to become part of Pete's legal team. Just like that. Pete was almost shocked. "Isn't that unethical?"

"I defer to you on that."

Pete was dumb, he really was, but even he was smart enough to avoid entanglement with Tuttle. Besides, his own lawyers, Cutt and Curran, would not have accepted Tuttle. Not that they were much better. Curran had suggested to her, just before the final arguments in Pete's divorce actions, that she might want to talk over things in the near future.

"Things?"

"I think you know what I mean. A man can express his intentions in many ways other than a formal will."

Meaning that Pete had told Curran. She felt betrayed, although she shouldn't have. Even while she was telling Pete, she knew it was a mistake. It was not the kind of secret you could trust a Peter Rush with. But she let him know what she thought of him, in no uncertain terms. Just in time. He had actually authorized Curran to allude to her and Mr. Farley in his final remarks.

"If he does, I will kill you."

"Why not? You don't owe them. They owe you."

"I won't discuss it. Tell him not one whisper, do you understand?"

He understood. Big as he was, she felt at that moment she could crush him to death in her arms, activated by fury. Little-bitty women have been known to lift trucks to free their children. That is how she felt then, and Pete must have known it. He agreed. But already one other person knew and that person was a lawyer. She had let a genie out of the bottle and did not know how to get it in again. Pete might be dead now, but Curran knew.

Cadbury, too, of course. And Liz Farley. For heaven's sake, she might as well rent the Goodyear blimp and advertise it to the world. I was Harold Farley's mistress for ten years. She smiled sadly. But the thought of another line chased the fantasy away. We had a child with spina bifida and let him die. That was between her and God. No one knew of that. No one. Not even Amos Cadbury. It was her most sacred memory, her dead child a link between her and Harold Farley, the two of them gone now past that bourn from which no traveler returns.

She arrived at the church at ten past and Father Dowling was just finishing a homily. He returned to the altar and June followed the liturgy with interest. Harold had explained the Mass to her, but she had seen it only a few times. This is the church in which he had gone to Mass every Sunday. It was an obligation. She liked the thought of him in church, praying for her as well as for his family.

The church was far from full now, maybe twenty people. Was it the nice weather outside? These people, mostly women, had the look of regulars. They would be here rain or shine.

It occurred to her that this was also the church where Pete Rush's funeral had been. The way the priest faced the church made it obvious why Father Dowling knew she had not been here then. Except that he wouldn't know who she was. People were getting out of their pews and she thought it was over, but they started toward the front and she realized it was to receive communion. This is what Harold had not been able to do.

"But who would know?"

"I would know," he used to say. "And God would know."

He had really believed in God. Religion wasn't just a lot of rules and the way he had been brought up. He had no doubt at all that there was a supreme being who made the world and everything in it and who came to earth as Jesus.

"I must answer to him eventually," he told her. "And so must you."

"Me? I haven't done anything wrong."

He smiled. "No, I don't think you have. Not in your heart."

"And neither have you!"

But there was no way in the world she could have convinced him of that. Loving her, wonderful as it was, even though God knew about it and somehow meant it to happen, was sinful. "For me," he had added.

"Then it is for me too."

"You make me feel guilty of Original Sin."

The Mass was over. When Father Dowling left the altar, the old women rose and gathered in groups and began whispering. What did they talk about? What does anyone talk about?

June got up and left the church to walk to the rectory and see what Father Dowling wanted to talk about. He certainly did not beat around the bush.

"Let me begin by telling you what the police now know."

"The police? How would you know what they know?"

The room they sat in was like the den Harold had made in the apartment. Full of books. And smoke. But Harold had not smoked.

"I just do. First, they know you were the one who picked up Timothy Rush from Mrs. Hospers. I mention that first because it is the least important. Mrs. Hospers identified you."

"When?"

"Let me put it all before you first. I am providing you with reasons why you should not go back to Dr. Dunn's office."

"How did you know I work there?"

"Does it matter? You know they found your lipstick in Peter Rush's office. The curiosity of Lieutenant Horvath was piqued."

She looked at him. She did not know why he was telling her this or how he had come to know it, but he had her attention.

"They know about the apartment in Evanston. They know of your affair with Mr. Farley. They know that he did not die as he was found."

"They were told then."

"No. Believe me, they were not. The only other person who could have *told* them has far more reason than you to keep it quiet."

She sat back. "I am going to smoke."

"So am I."

He lit a pipe, a nice-smelling tobacco, not too sweet. She had been smelling earlier versions of it since entering the room.

"You seem to know everything."

"Only because *I* have been told. But there is one thing I don't know and only you can tell me. Did you kill Peter Rush?"

"No!"

He looked at her for perhaps half a minute. "I believe you," he said finally.

"It's true!"

"I said I believe you. The police will be another matter."

—— Twenty-Six ——

June wasn't there. Dunn didn't know where she was and he said, looking over both shoulders, he was mighty pissed. "She's supposed to be back here at one."

"She's usually reliable?"

"It's her middle name." Then Dunn

205

had a thought. "Why do you want to see her?"

"We're still investigating the matter across the hall."

Dunn made a face. "A helluva thing to have happen. This location was supposed to be a good one. Will you look up and down that hallway? It's like a county fair. And Rush fit right in. Financial counselor! He tried to sell me a car."

"What kind?"

"Any kind I wanted. Preferably a luxury car. When I said I wasn't in the market, he said that was because I wasn't getting the right advice on my investments. The last advice I took I bought a condo in the Canary Islands. A lemon tree right outside my window. I should have known."

Keegan tried to think where the Canary Islands were. The Caribbean? What difference did it make?

"How well did you know Rush?"

"How well? I didn't know him at all. You didn't have to know him for him to come on with the big buddy act. 'If you're earning so much money, why aren't you rich?' That sort of thing. Cheerful. Too cheerful. I should relocate, but there is nothing worse for a practice than moving. I found that out when I moved here. The biggest mistake I ever made. I've lost patients."

"Did Rush have a lot of clients?"

"I didn't keep tabs on the man."

"But he was doing okay?"

"If wishes were horses, he was. An idea man. You know the type. But always small ideas. Have you ever noticed at Vegas the guys at the slot machines trying out some damned system they've devised? Imagine spending your time working out a system for slot machines." Dunn shook his head.

"It doesn't look like June's coming back," Cy said.

"Great."

"If she does, tell her we were here."

"I will tell her several things when she gets back."

At the door Cy turned. "Was June with you at your previous location?"

Dunn shook his head. "No. She was part of a clean start."

As they went down the stairs to the lower lobby, Keegan reflected that these must be the stairs on which the receptionist had seen Connie the day Rush was killed. What had Dowling suggested? She found the door locked and left. Okay. But why was she here at all? He put the question to Cy.

"Does she deny it?"

"Did we put it to her as a question?"

"If we do and she says she wasn't here, whose word do we take?"

"Ask Agnes."

"We going to see Cadbury now?"

"I want to talk to the manager of this place first."

With Cy and Hank Guardino and himself in the office, there wasn't much room left for the furniture. Keegan, prompted by Cy, alluded to Hank's athletic career.

Hank shook his head. "How 'bout them Bears?"

"Never would have believed it."

"You think it's catching?"

"For the Cubs?"

He made a face. "No. The Sox."

There are two classes of Chicagoans, Cub fans and Sox fans. God creates them that way. Reason has nothing to do with it. The wise fan recognizes this and, when in the vicinity of a fan of the opposite persuasion, changes the subject.

"You had any further thoughts on the Rush killing?"

"Only that it coulda hurt me more. Not much publicity, considering he was in the paper every day there for a while."

"Maybe they got tired of writing about him."

"You still don't know who did it?" Hank asked.

"Someone suggested the mob."

"Jesus."

Keegan said, "I know you've talked to other officers, but I wonder if you would give me a rundown on your morning on the day Rush was found."

"You mean what I did?"

"To the best of your recollection."

"What is this anyway?"

"Just routine."

Suddenly Hank was sweating. Had they stumbled on to something?

"Come on. Tell us your movements."

"She told you, didn't she?"

"We want to hear it from you."

Hank got out his handkerchief and began to use it as a towel on his sweaty hands. "Okay. And this is *all* that happened, okay? She called down and said she was worried. Rush didn't seem to be in his office. So what? She knew he had planned to be in early that morning, she said. Besides she had seen someone around that made her concerned."

"Someone."

"She never said who. I never asked. I figure now it was bullshit. Anyway we went up and opened the door and went in. You know what we found."

"What?"

"Aw, come on."

Keegan said, "The lieutenant asked you to describe what you and June saw when you entered Peter Rush's office."

"A body. We found his body."

"Was he still alive?"

"Don't tell me she said that. He was dead all right."

"How'd you feel about that?"

Hank got mad. "How'd I feel? I'll tell you how I felt. I felt like a sucker. That guy owed me. Rent. And he owed me personally."

"How?"

"I gave him good-faith money to get me a Caddie."

"You can make a claim against his estate."

"Sure. And next year a Cadillac will be delivered to my door."

"What did you take out of the office, Hank?" Cy's voice invited confidence.

Hank was sweating again. "Women. I shoulda known. She said, go ahead, take it, why not." He got up and waddled to a file cabinet and inched it open. Keegan looked at Cy. Hank reached in and brought out an envelope. He put it on the desk.

"Open it," Keegan said.

Hank took out a gold watch. Keegan extended his ballpoint, indicating Hank should hang the watch on it. He examined it. It was running. Battery-operated. Strange thought. Peter Rush dead and buried and here was his watch still keeping time.

"Anything else?"

"She told you it all, huh? Okay. I cleaned out his wallet. I got exactly forty dollars. I had given him two-fifty. He was repaying a debt. Something he had to be dead to do."

"How much money?" Cy asked.

"Forty bucks."

"What denominations?"

"Is something wrong with that money?" Hank looked as if he could believe anything now, so long as it meant bad luck for him.

"Hank, you still got it?"

He took out his billfold and looked at its contents. "It was two twenties. I don't know which ones."

"How many twenties you have?"

Hank counted them. "Six."

"Hank, you spent any since the day Rush paid you back?"

"A twenty?" He thought. "No. I'm sure I haven't."

"We better take those. They will be returned to you, of course, unless there is any question of their genuineness. Or any question that they belong to you."

"They gotta have my name on them?"

"Lieutenant Horvath will give you a receipt."

In the car, Keegan said, "Maybe it was chicken, but we can't have people mucking up the scene of a murder."

But Cy needed no convincing. He opened the envelope and looked at the twenty-dollar bills they had taken from Hank. "The root of all evil."

"That and sex."

"Yeah."

The woman at the receptionist desk in Cadbury's office reminded Keegan of a nun who'd taught him in seventh grade. He stood a little straighter when she looked up.

"Captain Keegan to see Mr. Cadbury."

"Is he expecting you?"

"I believe he is."

She looked at him just as that nun had long ago. "Then he must have forgotten. He is not in the office."

"Oh, that's a shame. When do you expect him back?"

"He didn't say when he would return."

"Did he tell you where he was going."

"He did."

"Where?"

"I do not give out that kind of information, gentlemen. I am surprised that you would ask." She was aware of Cy's effort to read the appointment book open before her and she closed it with a snap.

"If you would repeat your names, I will tell Mr. Cadbury you called."

"We'll be back. My name is Keegan. Would you like me to spell it?"

"Two *e*'s?"

"And one *n.*"

"I have never seen it spelled with two *n*'s."

"Neither have I. And this is Lieutenant Horvath."

"The purpose of your visit?"

It was one of those times when he was tempted to be cute. This woman—her name was Cleary, according to the nameplate on her desk—brought out the worst in him. Unflappable, condescending, and bland. How might she react if he said they had come about Harold Farley's autopsy? But even if that elicited a reaction from the Cleary woman, it would be small compensation for giving Cadbury the chance to prepare for their questions.

"Could you get anything from the appointment book?" he asked Cy in the elevator.

"It looked like Dowling's name."

"Dowling!"

"I'm pretty sure that's what she had written down."

—— Twenty-Seven ——

The idea to take June Slate to the Farleys was first prompted by his resolution not to involve Edna Hospers further, but as he dialed the number he felt that this bringing together of the two women in the life of Harold Farley was overdue. Suddenly June got to her feet.

"I'm not going there. I couldn't."

"You can't stay here."

"I'll go to a motel then. Why not? That's what . . ."

He looked up but she did not finish the sentence. The Farley phone was ringing. Father Dowling held up his hand. Anxiety, curiosity, other less easily identifiable emotions flickered across her face. He did not fear she would leave the study. The phone continued to ring and June sat down. It had seemed an inspiration and he was reluctant to hang up, but eventually he did.

"We can try again."

"I wouldn't have gone there, so it doesn't matter."

"Sooner or later you will have to talk to the police, I suppose."

"Why? I didn't do anything."

"And in theory at least, you don't have to prove that. But you now know all the circumstantial evidence they have. Inevitably they will act on it. When that happens you will have to confute the evidence. Prove your innocence, that is, no matter the theory."

"Or they might find who did kill Pete."

"Constance Farley Rush?"

"I know she was there. And talk about motive! If I were her, I would have killed him months ago. But they arrested her and then let her go. Why? Because there is no evidence she was inside the office. Do they think she was never in it? That's nonsense. She chose it for him and furnished and decorated it. Fingerprints? Even I would know enough to wear gloves if I were going to do something like that."

"But why would she have waited so long?" Father Dowling asked. "You yourself said it. If she were going to kill him, she would have done it before or during the time he was parading their private affairs through the newspapers."

She moved her hands to a new position on her purse. "Maybe he threatened to do worse."

"What do you mean?"

"You know about Mr. Farley and me. That was not common knowledge. Harold called us the best-kept secret since Linear B."

"An erudite comparison. Did you understand the allusion?"

"He explained it to me." Her chin lifted. "He was my teacher as well as my lover. I suppose the sort of arrangement we had sounds sordid, particularly the way it ended. He had a saying, a kind of prayer, 'Let my life end in tragedy if it must, but do not let it end in farce.' He might have been fearing what finally happened." She shuddered. "It is a terrible thing to have to handle the dead body of someone you loved. Taking him out like that, the way one takes out the trash. Life is a terrible thing in the end, isn't it?"

"There is a formula we use when putting ashes on the forehead at the beginning of lent."

"*Mamento, homo, quia pulvis es . . .*" She faltered, closed her eyes, moved her lips in an effort to remember.

Father Dowling said, "*Et in pulverem reverteris.* Remember, man, that thou art dust and into dust thou shalt return. Did he teach you that?"

"He hoped I would become a Catholic. But not yet. His great hope and prayer was to be reconciled with the Church."

"Let us hope he is reconciled with God."

"He was a good man, Father. I don't mean just that he was good to me, though he was. He wanted me to be good, to be educated, to take pleasure in worthwhile things. We weren't just using one another. Can that be bad?"

"Evil isn't a thing, you know. It's an illicit use of something good. I am sure there were many good things in your relationship."

"He hated that word used that way."

Father Dowling smiled. "So do I. I resisted it for a long time, but in the kind of work I used to do, people said it so often that resistance became impossible. One day I heard myself saying it and it seemed pedantic to fight it."

"What kind of work was that?"

"The Church has her own law and courts. I was a member of the marriage court."

"The one that gives annulments?"

Was that the common understanding now? It was no longer fair, not after John Paul II, but there had been a period when some courts—not the Chicago one—had doled out annulments on the flimsiest of bases. Remembering the anguish he had felt listening to the pleas of people caught in impossible but valid marriages, Roger Dowling could understand how a court might be overcome with compassion. But feelings cannot change facts, and a valid marriage is a valid marriage. An annulment says that a marriage never existed because of well-defined impediments. Lax courts had introduced dubious psychological impediments, apparently reasoning that if a marriage went bad it had not been meant to be in the first place.

June said, "I read of one in the paper. Was it Frank Sinatra's? I suggested to Harold that he get one. I never brought it up again.

"He was angry?"

"Worse. He was saddened almost to the point of tears. He said that would be like denying he had ever loved me. He was married for life. And he told me I was free to leave him whenever I wished."

"Did you ever consider that?"

"Father, neither of us had any idea he was going to die. We both thought of things going on as they were for years. Whenever we talked of changes, they were far off in the future. He was much older than I, but he was not an old man."

"Did Peter Rush remind you of him?"

"Good Lord, no. They were as different as two men could be."

"Yet you were attracted to Rush."

"Attracted? Maybe fascinated. Why do people go to horror movies? Why are people fascinated by baboons at the zoo? I had never known anyone like him, someone without a sense of shame. I came to know him, yes. We had dinner together a few times and talked a lot. We had the Farleys in common, you see. Two outsiders. It was as if we had a common goal."

"Getting money from them?"

She frowned. "Harold intended to leave me money. He told Mr. Cadbury that, but apparently just as a point of information. He had not yet changed his will when he died. The biggest mistake I ever made in my life was telling Pete that. His theory was that the Farleys were stingy. He said this once too often about Harold and to defend him I blurted out that he wasn't like that at all. I knew." She looked abject. "That was all, but I should have known it was more than enough for someone like Pete. I'm really not surprised the police have found out what they have. Peter Rush figured it out first."

"Linear B was readable at last."

"Yes. And knowledge was power to Pete. He began to treat me as a collaborator. A co-conspirator. I pretended we had a common interest because of what he knew. But I was determined to prevent him from using it."

She said it simply as a matter of fact. She was determined to protect the good name of the late Harold Farley and of his family.

"But Pete did not keep it to himself, Father. Several lawyers have contacted me, wanting me to sue the Farley estate."

"You've refused?"

"Of course."

"But say he had changed his will, say he died a natural death. Wouldn't his family have learned of you then?"

"He said no. He meant to work it out in such a way that even then it would be a secret. He had a very good lawyer."

"Mr. Cadbury."

"Amos Cadbury."

"If financial arrangements could be made now, with similar discretion, would you be interested?"

She looked closely at him. "Why do you ask?"

"I think such arrangements could be made."

"You've been talking to Mr. Cadbury."

"Let's say he's been talking to me."

June shook her head slowly. "No. I've thought about it and decided I don't want money. What would it make me if I took money now? And it was a lesson seeing what greed was doing to Pete. I don't want to be like that. Pete really believed that if his income were double, triple, quadruple what it was, he would be happy and life would be utterly different. His idea of happiness was a more expensive car, a more expensive apartment. Things. He had no mind at all."

Father Dowling knocked the contents of his pipe into the ashtray. "You say Mr. Farley spoke to you of Catholicism?"

"He wanted me to become a Catholic someday. But not as a favor to him. It was clear to me that being a Catholic was the most important thing in his life."

"Didn't you find that inconsistent with what we will not call your relationship?"

"It seemed to explain the inconsistency too."

"Have you thought about the Church?"

"Off and on. But whenever I do there's something in the news I know would have annoyed Harold and I forget it."

"Maybe we can talk about it sometime."

"We already are, aren't we?" She looked steadily at him. "I could never become one if I had to believe Harold Farley ended up in hell."

"You would not. You would be advised not to think it and to pray for his soul."

"I already do. . . . He gave me these."
She opened her bag and drew forth a rosary
that looked like jewelry.

"Do you use it?"

"Yes."

The phone rang and he let Marie take
it in the kitchen, but in a moment she
buzzed and he picked up the phone.

"Elizabeth Farley is on the line, Father."

"Hello. This is Father Dowling. I've been
trying to reach your mother."

"That's why I'm calling, Father. She's
suffered some kind of attack and I've taken
her to the hospital. Could you come?"

"I'll be there right away." He hung up.

June stood before he did. "Something has
happened?"

He told her. "Maybe you should go to
a motel after all."

She shook her head. "No, Father. What's
the point? I have nothing to hide."

—— Twenty-Eight ——————

Tuttle felt that sometimes it is necessary
to anticipate the future.

June had not definitively turned down
his offer to act as her counsel. He had it

223

on his father's authority that a woman's no is always equivocal. So he decided to proceed on the assumption that, once he got the ball rolling, she would be happy to come aboard. And step one, as he saw it, was to pay a visit to the Farley lawyer, the man who, along with Mrs. Farley, acted as executor of the estate: Amos Cadbury.

To say that Tuttle and Amos Cadbury were not on good terms would suggest that they were on some terms at all, and the fact is that if Cadbury had ever acknowledged his existence, Tuttle had missed it. People like Cadbury gave him a pain in the you-know-what, acting as if they were aristocrats, while groundlings like Tuttle were beneath notice. This is a democracy, isn't it? Rank should be a matter of merit rather than luck or birth.

Nevertheless, Tuttle stood in awe of Cadbury's supreme self-possession. He had observed Cadbury during the Rush divorce, and "cool" was too hot a term to describe his manner. Impervious, that was the word. Cadbury was impervious to events and people whose existence he chose not to acknowledge. His polite and gallant manner to Judge Jones was like a shouted rebuke, but of course she did not notice. She belonged to the new aristocracy of assertion. If you told people loudly enough that they owed you something, chances are it would pay off, if only as a way to shut you up. That is how Molly Jones got her judgeship.

Tuttle decided it would be unwise to call ahead and announce his coming. It went without saying that if he asked for an appointment, Cadbury's calendar would be found unable to accommodate him. The thing to do was to show up and brazen his way into the inner sanctum, resolved from the outset to do whatever he had to in order to get face-to-face with Cadbury.

But riding up in the elevator he had misgivings. Besides, an idea had struck. Could he wangle a writ from Judge Jones forcing Cadbury to attend a hearing? But even Judge Jones would want proof that Tuttle was representing June. He decided he was doing the right thing. However outrageous his behavior, he could be certain Cadbury would not report him to the bar association. That would entail acknowledging that Tuttle existed.

The elevator stopped, the door opened, and there stood Captain Keegan and Lieutenant Horvath.

"You move your office?" Horvath asked.

Keegan gave Tuttle a fierce look. He had the memory of an elephant and they had crossed paths many times. "You still practicing law, Tuttle?"

"No. I decided to quit working and become a cop."

Horvath's massive hand was keeping the elevator door open. "You want a client, you might check on the manager of the Fenwick Mall. Guardino."

"Yeah?" Who could tell when Horvath was joking?

"He may want to bring an action."

"What charge?"

"Police brutality."

Tuttle got out of the car and the two cops got in.

"I'll tell Hank you sent me," Tuttle said to the door when it was closed.

At least this chance meeting had given him an opener. Tuttle sailed into Cadbury's outer office, looking from left to right. "Haven't they arrived?"

"I beg your pardon?"

"Two police detectives. Keegan and Horvath."

"They just left."

Tuttle made an impatient noise and

pulled off his tweed hat. It was getting a little warm to be wearing that, but he considered it good luck. "Did they make the arrest?"

"The arrest!"

"I'd better talk to Mr. Cadbury before it's too late."

"I haven't the faintest idea what you're talking about."

"Of course you don't. They wouldn't tell you a thing like this. Is that Cadbury's office?"

She rose like a flight of birds as he started around her desk.

"Stop!"

"He has nothing to fear from me."

She gave him an arctic look. "Mr. Cadbury does not fear anybody. And neither do I."

"Perhaps you don't recognize me."

"I do not."

"I am a fellow lawyer."

"I am not a lawyer."

"I meant of Mr. Cadbury."

"He would have to be the judge of that."

"I have to see him. For his sake as well as mine."

"You wish to be a client of Mr. Cadbury?"

Tuttle smiled and nodded. Why not? Any way he could get it, he would take.

"Who recommended you?"

He could see this was the beginning of another runaround.

"June Slate."

"I don't know the name."

"Mr. Cadbury does. Tell him I mentioned that name."

"And what is your name?"

Oh, the hell with it. "Judge Jones," he said, and headed for the elevator. Maybe he could salvage something by talking to Keegan and Horvath. He wondered if they had gotten past old granite face.

Horvath was seated behind the wheel of a car parked on the street below and Keegan was beside him, talking on the radio. Tuttle was just pushing through the revolving doors as Horvath pulled away from the curb. On impulse, Tuttle hailed a cab. The driver was Hispanic and had trouble with Tuttle's English. In sign language as much as anything, Tuttle told him to "follow that car."

It would have been just his luck if they had headed for City Hall, but Horvath took a left and then a right, and Tuttle pulled at the brim of his hat and smiled. They were going out to St. Hilary's, he would bet on it. They ought to put Dowling on the payroll and give him an office downtown—it would save the taxpayers a lot of mileage. Maybe he would look up Tom Pouce when he was out there. That would be his excuse for being in the neighborhood.

What did he expect to learn? His antennae had been twanging ever since the elevator opened and he looked out at the two cops. They were onto something, and since the murder of Peter Rush was on the platter, it could well be that. It had not escaped Tuttle that the Fenwick Mall was where Rush had his office. They had probably just come from there. But why the stop at Cadbury's? Tuttle groaned. His antennae did not always signal good news for him, and he had the fear he might lose the chance of representing June Slate when she made her claim against the Farley estate.

Imagine Farley keeping a girl in Evanston for years. It was like trying to imagine Cadbury snuggling with some floozy. All flesh is grass, as the poet says, and Tuttle was not about to be surprised by the antics of men.

It just showed you these aristocrats were human. No. That was undeserved praise.

He got out of the cab in front of the church while Horvath turned the corner to park at the rectory. "How many pesos?" he asked the driver.

A brown finger pointed at the meter. The guy must have done the dog paddle across the Rio Grande, Tuttle thought. He gave him a five and waved him off. Bread upon the water. *El pan sobre la agua.*

He shouted that after the cab, part of the Tuttle Good Neighbor policy.

When he looked around the corner of the church, he saw Keegan and Horvath barreling out to their car. He ran after them, trying to catch their attention, but they took off.

Breathless, Tuttle stopped on the sidewalk and then noticed a woman standing in the rectory door. The housekeeper, old what's-her-face. He walked swiftly to her.

"Was that Captain Keegan?"

"Yes, Mr. Tuttle, it was."

"Ah, you remember me, Mrs. . . . ." He appealed for help.

"Murkin."

"Right."

"He wasn't here a minute."

Tuttle sighed. "Then he must have received word."

"I gave it to him."

Tuttle looked receptively at her, praying that another adage of his father was right. It was.

"They went to the hospital," Mrs. Murkin said. "St. Jude's. Mrs. Farley was taken there a short time ago."

"May I use your phone, Mrs. Murkin? I have to call a cab."

—— Twenty-Nine ——

When Roger Dowling arrived at the hospital, Sister Juliana was at the front desk and, hearing him ask for Mrs. Farley, turned and put out her hand.

"Oh good, you're here. I'll take you to her room."

"She's in a room?"

"In intensive care, Father. I'm sorry it's always someone's being ill that gives me a chance to see you."

Sister Juliana was in her early seventies, looked fifty and was a product of the golden age of the Church in America, when convents bulged with the religious and there was no difficulty finding nuns to teach in the parochial schools and run the hospitals. It was their contribution that had made the system economically feasible. Sister Juliana had gone through a demanding novitiate, been introduced to a life of prayer and of service to others. And of course her respect for priests was total—impersonal, but total. They were men ordained to carry on the work of Christ.

"How long have you been at St. Jude's, Sister?"

"Oh, I stopped counting long ago."

Vanity? He doubted it. "How long has it been since you quit counting?"

Her cheeks dimpled when she smiled but her eyes did not alter. Roger Dowling had the sudden sense that this woman had an intense and profound spiritual life.

"I came here directly from the novitiate, but after seventeen years I was assigned to a parish as school nurse. Blessed Sacrament. When the school closed, I was sent back here." That simple itinerary would have covered a host of anguishing changes in the life she had embraced as a girl. It would be interesting to ask Sister Juliana what she thought of the new nuns.

"How serious is Mrs. Farley's condition, Sister?"

"It was a stroke. It seems likely that she will live but God only knows with what damage."

"I see."

"Her daughter brought her in. If the mother is anything like her, she will pull through."

She meant Liz, and Liz looked out from the room as he came down the hall. Sister Juliana had stopped at the huge circular desk that formed the hub of a wheel of rooms. The patients could be constantly monitored, by machine and visually. Jeremy Bentham had thought prisons should be like this.

"She wants the last sacraments, Father," Liz said. "Just now things look slightly better, but I don't think she will relax until she's received them."

Mrs. Farley lay on her back in bed, silver hair and white face against the white linen. She had become very quickly old. But her eyes sparkled when he came in. He took her hand and pressed it, then put on his stole. He motioned Liz to stand on the other side of the bed, and then they began the prayers for the dying. One of the deepest satisfactions of being a parish priest, after all those years as a bureaucrat, was that now he regularly dispensed the sacraments. He could have counted the times he had given the last rites before coming to St. Hilary's. His one regret was that there weren't as many baptisms as funerals in the parish, but even that had begun to change, as younger people moved into St. Hilary's.

Mrs. Farley kept her eye on him throughout and when he anointed her hands and feet and eyes and ears, the senses with which she had offended God, she closed her eyes, at peace and still alive. The effect of the last sacraments is often to put a patient on the road to recovery, and whether this was psychological or something else did not matter. The psychological necessarily involved faith in the efficacy of the sacrament.

He moved away from the bed and Liz came around to him. "That is the first time she has voluntarily closed her eyes."

"What have they told you?"

She made a face. "As little as possible. Do they all live in dread of malpractice suits, or what?"

"Sister Juliana told me she didn't think there is mortal danger now."

Liz tugged at his sleeve and they moved out of the room. Over her shoulder he could see the nurses and interns busy at their work. It looked like the flight deck of a spaceship.

"There will be damage from the stroke, Father. Did you notice her mouth?"

He lifted his brows in answer.

"The left corner is tugged down. I don't think she has any feeling on her left side."

"Whatever lies ahead, the Farleys can handle it."

Fire sparked in her eye. "Yes, we can."

"If you have to go to your office, I will stay with her."

"Connie ought to be here."

"Well, the baby . . ."

"The baby! She will see as much of her child as the Queen of England saw of hers. One thing about Mother. *She* raised us."

"Not your father?"

She smiled. "He raised *her.* . . . On the phone you said you had been trying to reach us."

"I wanted to ask your mother to grant someone asylum."

Liz turned her head slightly. It reminded

Father Dowling of June Slate. "A Latin American?"

"No. A local girl named June Slate."

The effect on Liz was immediate. She might have had a stroke herself the way she stiffened. She had looked away from Father Dowling and she stayed that way.

"That is not funny, Father."

"She is the prime suspect in your brother-in-law's murder now that Connie has been released."

"It is simply out of the question."

"Because of your mother's illness?"

"No!"

"Liz, I know your reason. Mr. Cadbury came to me . . ."

She turned. "That fool! He had no right."

"He asked me to intervene with June to see if she would accept a settlement from the Farley estate, as your father wanted."

Liz shut her eyes very tight. "Father Dowling, this is a very painful subject for me. Apparently you know about it. Imagine what it is like for a daughter to learn something like that of her father."

"Agonizing."

She opened her eyes. "It is! I don't think

236

I can ever forgive him. I wonder if God can."

"You know better than that."

She smiled in a way that seemed to hurt her lips. "As a good little Catholic I should know better? My father was a prominent Catholic layman, wasn't he? It said so in all the obituaries. Honors, activities, on and on. And all the while he was sleeping with that girl in Evanston."

He could understand that knowledge of her father's infidelity had been an earthquake. The pride she felt in being a Farley must have been learned from him. And then to find he had been keeping a girl more or less her own age. Yes, that must have been devastating. He wondered when her hair had turned gray. At her age it would have been natural to have something done to it, not that she wasn't striking-looking. She seemed to wear her silver hair defiantly, done in the same style as her mother's, as if she could not wait to be old. Yet often she wore a multicolored hat to Mass that all but concealed her hair.

"Surely you can't object to her being taken care of as your father wished."

"What I object to, Father Dowling, is that it will become public. Mr. Cadbury thinks he can conceal it. Well, my father thought he had concealed his mistress, yet I discovered her by studying the books. The money doesn't matter. It's what it will do to our name!"

—— Thirty ——————————

Keegan hated hospitals worse than he hated morgues. This was the hospital in which his wife had died and, with her, the real point of living. People had thought him phlegmatic toward his wife, hardly a sentimental lover, but he had been happiest when he was with her, and she had known it. And then she died.

It didn't make a lot of sense, but he blamed the hospital and the doctors and just about everyone who had tried to help her. No wonder doctors are always being sued. It's a natural reaction.

He let Cy go to the desk and find out where Mrs. Farley was. Intensive care. What else?

But she was still alive.

They had remodeled a lot in recent years, and that made it easier. He would not have recognized intensive care. And then he bumped into Elizabeth Farley, literally. She came barreling along, head down, and when she looked up at him, startled, there were tears in her eyes. And, for a moment, something akin to terror.

"How is she?"

"Father Dowling is with her now."

"She'll be all right," he said, drawing on that vast fund of idiotic remarks that seem available at such times. Elizabeth Farley looked at him. If she had hit him, he would not have complained.

"When did you bring her in?" Cy asked.

She looked at her watch, happy to have an excuse to be precise. "It's been nearly three hours."

"She call you or what?"

"No. I called home and didn't get an answer. I knew she was there so I tried again, and then I began to worry."

Keegan left Cy with Liz. Cy had a way with him, no doubt of that, asking just the right questions, no phony attempts to reassure her.

Roger Dowling stood at the foot of the bed, hands grasping the stainless-steel railing, eyes closed. Keegan hesitated in the doorway. After half a minute, he cleared his throat and Roger turned.

"I dropped by the rectory and Marie told me."

"Ah."

"Have you given her the last rites?"

"Yes."

Keegan forced himself to go near the bed and look at Mrs. Farley. She looked small and old, and there was a stiffness in the way she lay that he did not like.

A nurse came in and pushed him aside to peer at the monitor mounted over the bed. Mrs. Farley was wired every which way. He was still in the nurse's way.

"Let's wait outside," he suggested to Roger.

Outside, Keegan saw that Cy was still talking to Liz. "How does it look, Roger?"

"They think she will pull through, but with some damage."

Keegan wanted no details. "Can we get a cup of coffee?"

The priest thought a moment. "Why not? I'll tell them at the desk I'll be downstairs."

"We're going for coffee," Keegan said when they passed Liz and Horvath.

"I'm going back to my office and close up," Liz said. "I just took off when I knew something was the matter with Mother."

"I'll stay with Mrs. Farley," Cy said.

"Thank you, Lieutenant." Cy had Liz's vote for man of the year.

In the cafeteria, they picked up cups of coffee at the counter and carried them to a table the size of a chessboard. Keegan lowered himself into a chair, certain it would not support him.

"I hate hospitals," he said.

"How is the case going?"

"Peter Rush? Well, you know what we know. Maybe not quite all. The manager of the Fenwick Mall went into the office and found Rush. June Slate called him. He thinks she suckered him into going in."

"Why?"

"He didn't say."

"It doesn't make much sense, does it?"

"Roger, why don't we just let things develop? Don't tell me why she could not possibly have done it. For all I know, Connie was inside the office that morning, too."

Roger had taken out his pipe and lit what was in the bowl. Not a very aromatic result. "You may be right."

Keegan shook his head. "The other day you were telling me she went to the office, found the door locked and left. And that is when June Slate saw her."

"Either could have happened."

"Or neither. We have only June Slate's word that Connie was there."

"Haven't you asked her?"

"She can't testify against herself," Keegan said, cheating a bit.

"But you have only Edna Hospers's word that June Slate picked up little Timothy from her." Roger's disappointment seemed directed at himself. "Why on earth would she have picked up the baby? How did she know where it was?"

"I'll ask her when I see her."

"When will that be?"

"Good question. She didn't show up for work this afternoon. We've alerted the airlines in case she tries to buy a ticket."

"She might take a train."

"Ha."

"Or a bus."

"Have you taken a look at a bus station recently?"

"I can't say that I have."

"The word that comes to mind is unsavory. Roger, in many ways this country is going to hell."

"No way to run a railroad?"

"That's true. Not that the railroads ever worked well. Do you know Tom Pouce? Of course you do. He has a railroad pension. He was a fireman for thirty years, most of them on a diesel that didn't need a fireman." Keegan threw up his hands.

"What are those letters they use in geometry?"

"ABC?"

"No. After the proof."

"QED?"

"That's it. What does it mean?"

"What you meant when you threw up your hands."

Keegan went back to intensive care with Roger.

"Liz is back," he said when they came out of the elevator and saw Cy in conversation with her. But when the woman turned, he saw it was Connie wearing a hat like her sister's. Her eyes were unblinking and wary as they approached, but it was Father Dowling she looked at.

"She's going to be all right, Father." She said it as if she expected to be contradicted.

"Everyone says so."

"Have you seen Liz?" Connie removed the hat.

"She was here when I gave your mother the last rites."

Connie tossed her hair. "Thank God for good old reliable Liz." Her eyes went to the center of the circular room and the activity there. "Liz would be right at home here." She glanced at Roger Dowling. "I should have checked on Mother. I should have been there to help her."

"The main thing is she was helped. You have your baby and your own life."

"My life. That's probably what brought this on. Dear God, the trouble I've been to her. Not just now. All my life." And she began to cry.

Keegan felt a lump in his throat and turned away, but only to face Horvath.

"Check downtown, Cy," he barked.

He himself went into Mrs. Farley's room, propelled almost against his will. It was as if he were proving to himself he was really tough as nails. When he stood beside the bed, Mrs. Farley's eyes opened and fixed on him. Her lips trembled and she seemed to chew them. He realized she was trying to talk. He leaned over the bed but all she could manage was a wheezing sound.

"Everything's going to be all right, Mrs. Farley."

The sound became an angry hum. He had done it again. He leaned closer.

"There won't be any more problems for the Farleys. I guarantee that."

She seemed to be trying to sit up and Keegan straightened. Then a sound broke from the dry lips. He wasn't sure what she had said. But it sounded like "Liz."

"She'll be fine, Mrs. Farley. Both girls will be fine."

He had made her angry again. She probably wanted Liz with her. Perhaps she didn't even know who he was. He went out and told Connie her mother wanted her.

"Did she ask for me?" Connie dashed into the room.

"Did she speak?" Roger Dowling asked.

"She tried. But I think she was saying Liz."

As Roger Dowling went in to the patient, Cy came across the circular area to Keegan.

"Agnes has arrested June Slate."

—— Thirty-One ——————

The news that June Slate had been arrested got to Tuttle instantaneously, thanks to Peanuts Pianone, and the little lawyer beat it over to the jail in the certainty that now she would become his client.

"Whaddya mean, she's your client?" Lynch sighted down his bulbous nose at Tuttle.

"Just tell her I'm here, will you?"

"Her lawyer's with her."

"Her lawyer!"

"Amos Cadbury."

Tuttle actually threw his Irish tweed cap on the floor and thought seriously of stomping on it. He had the irrational conviction that Cadbury was his nemesis, forever snatching away opportunities from his deserving hands.

"How the hell did he hear about it already?"

Entering the room, Detective Agnes Lamb recognized Tuttle, turned to leave, then thought better of it. She came up to him and said, "She mentioned your name when I made the arrest."

"Tell me about it."

"She wanted to call a lawyer so I said sure go ahead and then she didn't seem to know who her lawyer was. She turned and asked me if I knew a lawyer named Tuttle."

"Yeah?"

"I didn't deny it."

"Thanks a lot."

"It didn't matter. She picked up the phone then and dialed."

"Cadbury?"

"He was already here when I brought her in."

"Let me buy you a cup of coffee."

She thought about it, then shrugged. "Make it a beer and it's a deal."

Across the street he ordered beer himself. Mervel was at the bar as they settled into a booth, Agnes on one side, Tuttle on the other. Tuttle had to admit the case against June Slate looked bad, bad enough that he no longer envied Amos Cadbury his client.

June Slate had had some kind of affair going with Peter Rush. She worked right across the hallway from where he had been killed. Apparently she had conned the mall manager into discovering the body with her, thinking that would deflect suspicion from her. And she claimed Connie Rush had been at her husband's office that morning.

"Wasn't she?" Tuttle asked.

"We have only June Slate's word for it."

"What's the motive?"

"You need a motive to kill Peter Rush?"

"You do for a trial."

Agnes sipped her beer. "She wanted to shut him up."

Tuttle said, "You'll have to explain that to me."

"June Slate had been the mistress of Harold Farley for ten years. He kept her in an apartment in Evanston. Rush found out . . ."

"So did I," Tuttle said.

"Sure you did."

"I did. I tried to get her to sue the Farley estate. She wouldn't listen to me. I don't get it. She's protecting the Farley name?"

"June Slate is also the woman who picked up the Rush baby from Edna Hospers. You know about that?"

Tuttle shrugged, so Agnes went through the whole thing. The only new item was that the patrol officers who had covered the Farley home the night Agnes and Horvath went there with a warrant for Constance Rush had noticed June Slate casing the place.

"What does that mean?" Tuttle asked.

"She was in her parked car up the street from the house. They took down the tag number, and that was it; they were supposed to keep an eye on the house."

"How did she know the baby was with the Hospers woman?" Tuttle asked.

Agnes stopped her glass of beer on the

way to her mouth. "You'll have to ask her that."

"Did you?"

She smiled. "Until you asked I didn't think of it. Did you ever think of becoming a cop?"

"Only during Lent."

"What does that mean?"

Tuttle said, "Ask Peanuts."

Tuttle remembered he had left Peanuts in his office with the pizza Peanuts had brought along with the news of the arrest of June Slate. He wondered if there was any left. He slid out of the booth just as Mervel came over to the booth.

"Thank you, Agnes. I'll leave you with the press."

"You paying for my beer?"

"I'll get it," Mervel said, frowning at Tuttle.

"These reporters and their expense accounts." Tuttle said and slapped Mervel on the back. Good old Mervel. He would pay for Tuttle's beer, too. Well, why not? Who had put him onto this story?

⸺ Thirty-Two ⸺

Roger Dowling agreed that the case against June Slate looked strong. She had opportunity, she had motive, and apparently she had tried to divert attention from herself to others.

"After all, Roger, we have only her word that Connie was near her husband's office that morning."

"What does Connie say?"

"It no longer matters. Connie didn't do it."

"But, Phil, you have only Guardino's word that June Slate was in that office with him when he says he found the body. He had as much motive as anyone. And if exasperated debtors come into play, you will have a wide choice."

"June Slate is our choice."

"I think you're wrong."

Keegan was distracted by the television screen, where what Harry Caray thought was a home-run ball ended up in the left fielder's glove. He picked up his glass of beer and looked at his host. "Why?"

The priest's conviction was based on

June Slate's denial that she had killed Peter Rush when he asked her point blank in this very study. Not that he could expect that to persuade Phil Keegan.

"How did June Slate know Edna had the Rush baby, Phil?"

"I don't know."

"Have you asked her?"

"Cadbury has advised her not to say anything."

Roger Dowling tapped his pipe stem against his teeth. "I am surprised Amos took her case."

"So am I. It's not his kind of law."

"I was thinking of conflict of interest. His major concern will be the good name of the Farleys."

"Roger, that seems to have been June Slate's major concern as well. Curran tried to get her to sue the Farleys. So did Tuttle, not that it matters. She wouldn't do it."

"I'm not surprised."

"Well, that surprises me. I thought you were denying she had any motive to kill Peter Rush."

"What was her motive?"

"To stop his publicizing her affair with Harold Farley," Keegan replied.

"If Rush was going to do that, why

wouldn't he have used it in the divorce trial? He used everything else."

"And won everything he wanted? I wonder. Rush was malicious as well as unprincipled, apparently. And he also wanted June to get something from the Farleys. Maybe he thought making the affair known would remove June's reluctance to bring suit."

"You're guessing," said Roger Dowling.

"Suit yourself."

"The prosecutor thinks the case is strong enough to go to trial?"

"That's what he says, Roger."

"Would he have thought the same about prosecuting Connie?"

"You sound like Agnes Lamb."

"Would he?"

"You'll have to ask him, Roger. Are we going to watch this game or argue?"

They watched the game. The Cubs won. This cheered Phil, and the three bottles of beer he had didn't hurt his disposition either, so he was not irked when Father Dowling brought up June Slate again.

"Roger, if it makes you feel any better, I hope she wins too. I wish she had another lawyer than Cadbury. I don't like to see her going through this for a bum like Peter

Rush. Maybe she'll plead guilty to a lesser charge. God knows a jury could be made to sympathize with her. She could get off with a very light sentence."

"That is no consolation if she didn't kill Peter Rush."

June Slate agreed to see him when he went to the jail. She came into the visiting room looking almost bewildered. The sight of him seemed to cheer her.

"Mr. Cadbury says I can talk with you."

He smiled. "Why hasn't he asked for bail?"

"The judge hasn't ruled on it yet."

"Judge Jones?"

"I guess." She looked around. "Being here makes me feel guilty. I can understand why people confess to crimes they didn't commit."

"Don't you do that."

"Don't worry." She looked at him. "I am innocent, you know."

"I know."

"Because you take my word for it?"

"Yes. June, tell me something. You were the woman who picked up Timothy Rush from Edna Hospers?"

"Yes."

"And put him in a basket in the church and called me?"

She nodded.

"How did you know Edna Hospers had the baby?"

"Because I had planned to kidnap Pete's son the day before."

"You're not serious."

"It was the only thing he didn't get, custody of his son. He told me all kinds of lies about how his wife treated Timothy." A pause. "I lost a baby once, Father. Mine and Harold's. Timothy was Harold's grandson. That meant more to me than Pete's complaints. It was when he talked of kidnapping the baby that I got the idea. Pete didn't want his son, not really. He just wanted to spite the Farleys. Did his wife want the baby, really? I guess I thought they were two of a kind, and that seemed terrible for Harold's grandson."

"So you decided to take the baby?"

"Since neither one of them cared about it. If Solomon had given them the choice of dividing the baby, they might have agreed."

"You said you'd lost a baby."

Her eyes lifted and stared blankly at the wall behind him, growing moist.

She looked at him, hesitant. "It's a long story."

"We have all the time in the world."

Listening, aware of the agony this memory cost June, getting some intimation of what the experience itself must have been like, Roger Dowling's thoughts went to Harold Farley. What a price the man had paid for his affair with June Slate. Had she been his solitary lapse? There was no reason to think otherwise. That seemed the implication of Amos Cadbury's account of his friend's behavior. Farley had enjoyed the pleasure of lifting up June Slate, of being a benefactor as well as a lover. But he had paid in the coin of remorse of conscience, of duplicity, and then in the loss of his illegitimate son. And more than loss. He had decided the child should not be allowed to live. Dear God. And then to die in the wrong bed with all those sins upon his soul.

He stayed with June Slate for forty-five minutes, and even then had the feeling he was hurrying away.

"I'll be back."

"You must have many other things to do."

"You'd be surprised."

He drove back to the rectory, haunted by thoughts of that newborn baby allowed to die in an Evanston hospital. It would have been like Farley to have it baptized first. He hoped he had. The more Roger Dowling learned of Harold Farley, the more enigmatic and mysterious the man became.

Phil Keegan was there the night the matter of the baskets came up.

"Edna Hospers wants to know what she should do with the basket the baby came in," Marie said after supper, when she joined the pastor and Phil Keegan for coffee.

"Does she still have it?"

Marie nodded, dipping into her cup like a perpetual motion bird. "And I have the other."

"The other?"

"The second one."

"I don't understand."

"The one you brought him back from the church in the second time he was left there."

Keegan said, "Then you must have June Slate's basket, Marie. I'm going to have to take that one."

"You!"

"It's evidence."

"But of what, Phil? Even if you could prove the basket is hers . . ."

Roger Dowling stopped. Phil did not like that "if." There was no chance now he wouldn't take the basket with him when he went. Well, what did it matter really? June admitted she had picked up the Rush infant from Edna Hospers.

"If you want a basket, Marie, tell Edna to give you hers."

"What would I want with a basket? Besides, you're pretty generous with things belonging to Constance Farley Rush, aren't you?"

"Did you advise Edna to return her basket to Connie?"

"Should I?"

"You're the expert in stolen goods."

It was much later, nearly two in the morning, when Roger Dowling, nursing a final pipeful in his study, finally realized who had killed Peter Rush.

They had moved Mrs. Farley out of intensive care and into a double room whose second bed was for the moment unoccupied. Father Dowling drew a chair up next to the bed and took her hand in his. How gnarled and old it seemed, but then Mrs. Farley had aged years in a few days. Her gaunt lace was chalky against the pillow, and her silvery hair no longer shone. Her sunken eyes looked intently at him, and from time to time she worked her mouth and emitted an unintelligible sound. He asked her if she knew who he was. In response, her hand gripped his tightly and again she worked her mouth. Could he be sure that her mind was clear?

"Liz is at work, Mrs. Farley. She'll be here soon. You're better, you know. You're going to get well."

The expression in her eyes chided him and she relaxed her grip.

"Yesterday I visited June Slate in jail. She is still being held without bail." There was no reaction from the old woman.

"Do you know who June Slate is, Mrs. Farley?"

Her eyes held his almost hypnotically. Her chin dropped twice.

"You know everything?"

Again the chin touched her bony chest.

"June Slate is accused of killing Peter . . ."

Before he finished, she stiffened, then

tried unsuccessfully to talk. But the only way she could communicate was by answering his questions.

"How we doing?" asked a bright voice, imperfectly subdued by an effort to whisper. The nurse came to the bed, smiled down at Mrs. Farley, then looked at Father Dowling. "I hope I'm not interrupting."

"I'm not sure she even knows who I am."

"Don't kid yourself," the nurse said. "You should hear the stories they tell when they come out of these things. The comatose, too. We think they're way off on Cloud Nine, but you'd be surprised what they're aware of. Visitors are important."

So much for the hope that he could leave the question unanswered. The nurse left and Mrs. Farley closed her eyes. The priest leaned over the bed.

"Was it Liz, Mrs. Farley?"

The eyes opened and he felt swallowed in their depths. He waited for the pressure of her squeeze. It did not come.

"Was it Liz?"

She did not squeeze his hand. Her eyes closed then but she did not relax. Perhaps she did not understand after all. More likely she did and would not say. The mention of June Slate had drawn a strong reaction.

The mention of Liz had not. But he did not think that he was mistaken. He looked down at the old lady for a few minutes more, then left the room.

Entering the hallway, he started toward the elevators and saw Connie coming toward him. But when she pulled off the hat she was wearing, he realized it was Liz. No matter that he felt a fleeting cowardly impulse to go the other way, to avoid this, but she had already seen him.

"How's Mom?"

He took her arm. "She's resting now. Why don't we go to the visitors room."

"It's good of you to come see her, Father," Liz said, watching him light his pipe.

"The nurse thinks her mind is clear."

"I wonder."

"I'm sure of it."

She seemed wary. "I think it's a bit like parents imagining their babies talk."

"She can indicate yes and no."

Liz said nothing.

"I found that out when I told her of June Slate."

"You brought that woman up at a time like this?" Liz was furious.

"Your mother doesn't think June killed Peter Rush."

Liz made a noise. "How could she know one way or the other?"

"I think she knows who the killer is."

Liz was still angry with him. "And she told you?"

One can lie by remaining silent. He said nothing.

Her anger was replaced by wariness. "She can't speak. She can't say anything."

"She can answer questions."

"Yes and no?"

"Will you come with me while I ask her?"

The sounds and smells of the hospital seemed an unreal background.

"How did you know?"

"It's the hats you both wear. With them on, you could be twins. That's why June Slate thought it was Connie she saw that morning. But it was you, wasn't it? Connie had been seen in too many places that morning. There was no time for her to be at Pete's office too."

He waited. Liz seemed almost relieved to be discovered. He repeated his question. "It was you, wasn't it?"

"I went to his office." Her voice was not much more than a whisper, a penitent's voice. "We quarreled. I struck him with an ashtray. Just once. It was so easy."

"What did you quarrel about?"

"Amos Cadbury thought we should buy off June Slate. I did not. But Pete was egging that woman to sue the estate. Either way, the risks were too great."

"Risks."

"My father's deeds would have become public, shouted in the newspapers, babbled about on television . . ."

Her voice trailed off, as if she had just realized that such revelations were guaranteed, not prevented, by the death of Peter Rush.

"Are you going to call the police?"

"Perhaps you should call them, Liz."

"You mean it will look better to turn myself in?" She seemed to find it in keeping with the Farley code. "I will call Amos Cadbury, too."

She got to her feet, left the room, and set off down the hallway. Watching her, wondering if she would just keep on going, he saw her stop at the desk, ask to use the phone, and begin to dial.

She turned and looked back at him.

She might have been bidding farewell to the world.

He had not expected to feel triumphant—how could he possibly feel that?—but neither had he expected this odd suspicion that it was Liz who had caught him, and not the reverse.

Phil Keegan came alone, bringing the news that June Slate had been released on bond by Judge Molly Jones. It was clear to Roger Dowling that Phil would need a lot more than Liz's word before dropping the indictment against Dunn's receptionist. He did not want to leave the hospital until he knew what Phil would make of Liz's confession. Why did he hope he would not believe her?

Liz stood when Phil came into the visitors room as if welcoming her executioner. She was acting as a Farley should. What she had done was meant to protect the family name.

That was still her motive.

Her main concern was to preserve her father's good name. The dutiful daughter.

Of course!

Roger Dowling went swiftly down the hall to Mrs. Farley's room.

Her eyes were open and they widened when she saw him standing at the end of the bed. Again he took the chair beside the bed.

"Liz is here."

The eyes had followed him while he sat and they were watchful still.

"The police are talking to her."

The message calmed her and for a moment he wavered.

"Did Liz kill Peter Rush?"

The question transformed her. She trembled and managed to raise her head from the pillow. There was the look of one betrayed in her eye. No wonder. Her daughter was taking on the guilt and there was nothing she could do about it.

He said, "It was you, wasn't it, Mrs. Farley?"

Immediately, she calmed down. Her eyes were suddenly clear as a girl's. He took her hand.

"You killed Peter?"

A confirmatory squeeze. He had put the right question at last. Looking into those limpid eyes, Father Dowling had no doubt he had discovered the truth.

"I absolved you when I gave you the last rites, I absolved you of all your sins."

Half of her mouth responded with a smile.

Roger Dowling sat with her for a few minutes more, then got up and went down the hall to the visitors room.

"Phil, bring Liz with you. Mrs. Farley has something important to say."

—— Thirty-Three ——————

Mrs. Farley's prints matched some picked up by the mobile lab unit in Peter Rush's office the day he was found murdered. Not that it mattered. A second stroke took the old lady and she departed this vale of tears with the grim satisfaction of knowing that no one else would be blamed—or given credit—for killing Peter Rush.

"Mr. Cadbury would not let us talk with him while the divorce trial was on," Liz Farley said, "and she was anxious to confront him. She insisted on talking with him alone, so after we got to Pete's office, I left her there." Liz's mouth formed an odd smile. "I thought he wouldn't be safe with me and that it was better that Mom talk to him."

"Were you wearing a hat?" Father Dowling asked.

She nodded.

"That's why June Slate mistook you for Connie."

Liz winced at the name; she did not want to talk of her father's mistress. And who could blame her? It was sufficient that she had dropped her objections to the financial settlement Amos Cadbury worked out for June.

Phil Keegan was happy he did not have to see a Farley go on trial for murder, and it was a kind of celebration when he came to the rectory to watch the second game of a doubleheader on Channel 9. He took the beer Marie brought him and caught her hand before she left the study.

"How you fixed for baskets?"

"Collection baskets?"

"Clothes baskets. The kind people abandon babies in."

"Where is the one you confiscated, Phil Keegan?"

"We finally identified the person who bought it."

"Who?" Marie was tempted to sit, but remained standing. The smoke-filled study was not for her.

"B. F. Tuttle."

"Tuttle! The lawyer?"

Keegan looked at Father Dowling. "Aren't you surprised?"

"It always amazes me what you policemen can find out."

"But what on earth is his connection with the Rush baby?"

Phil sipped his beer. "Probably none. He said the basket had been stolen."

"By June Slate?"

"He isn't interested in bringing charges, so we didn't ask her. I left it on the porch. There's no baby in it."

Marie went to retrieve it. When she came back they were absorbed in the ball game so she humphed and went back to her kitchen.

June Slate had told Father Dowling of Tuttle's suggestion that she pick up the baby at Edna's.

"He wanted you to kidnap it?"

She smiled. "He's incredible. He said it's already kidnapped. He actually brought a clothes basket to Dr. Dunn's office."

"And you used it when you picked up the baby?"

"But I was acting on my own. Not because of Tuttle. I got cold feet as soon as

I had the little guy in the car. The smartest thing I ever did was to leave him in the church and call you."

She had given Dunn notice, but the dentist intended to relocate and said he would have let her go anyway. She didn't believe him, but it made it easier.

"Will you have to work now?"

"I may again, later. Just now I think of myself as on vacation. I'm reading."

"What?"

"Church history."

"Any time you want to talk, I'm here."

He left it at that. He didn't want her to think he was a clerical Tuttle.

On the screen, a well-hit ball made it into the bleachers. But there was no joy at the ball park or in the study of the St. Hilary rectory. The batter was on the visiting team.